Duty and Deception Series

BY
JL Redington

© JL Redington 2015

No part of this publication may be reproduced, or stored in a retrieval system, or transmitted in any form or by any means, electronic, mechanical, photocopying, recording or otherwise without written permission of the author.

Table of Contents

Prologue
Chapter One
Chapter Two
Chapter Three
Chapter Four
Chapter Five
Chapter Six
Chapter Seven
Chapter Eight
Chapter Nine
Chapter Ten
Chapter Eleven
Chapter Twelve
Chapter Thirteen
Epilogue
Preview

Prologue

Neo and Cayman sat at the conference table with the list of rogue team members before them. Neo struggled with the names on the page before him; amazed at the concept that this list of seemingly generic names could wreak such chaos in another human being's life. His life. He forced himself to read each name.

Tristan Bradford, Wesley Tipton (the word 'deceased' was written in large letters next to this name), Raymond Mathens, Aram Lincoln, Adrian Newberg, Abe Spencer, Drew Baldwin, Gus Atkinson, Ethan Williams, Harrison Hatchler.

He read the list over and over, recognizing several names on it as individuals he'd worked with, remembering laughing with them and cracking jokes, sitting at stakeouts back when they were all new with the FBI and they hadn't yet transferred to the NSA. His most disturbing memory was that of covering each other's backs in dangerous situations. What happened to these guys? The scope of devastation they were responsible for still left him astounded. *I should be over this by now. I should be handling this better, shouldn't I?*

Neo remembered Leon telling him in one of his sessions, "Don't should on yourself." He was 'shoulding' all over himself at this moment. He couldn't help but wonder how he'd missed the traitor in these men. Had he not been paying attention? Neo was in good company. No one in the Bureau or the NSA possessed even the slightest clue what this rogue group was doing. This had been a well-hidden, well-executed op, and he was the focus of it.

"You okay?" Neo looked up to see Cayman staring at him with concern.

"Oh, yeah, I was just thinking about these guys. I still have a really hard time reconciling what these men did."

"I'd be willing to bet you'll not reconcile any part of that for years to come. What I say we need to do is get started on this list. What do you think?"

Neo lifted his copy of the rogue team members off the table and held it before him. "Good idea. Tomorrow morning, yes? First thing."

"First thing."

The two men began early that next day, working quickly to get the needed evidence for the arrests they were about to make. The next two weeks would be busy, but hopefully very productive.

Chapter One

Tristan Bradford lay in bed; the beauty beside him very still, eyes closed. He rolled onto his side and admired her, outlining the shape of her perfect lips with his finger and then tracing the outline of her jaw. He sighed and rolled onto his back. Strange, how good it felt to have someone to tell his escape plan to. It clarified the weak places in his thinking and helped him find ways around the holes in his view of things. She'd been invaluable. How it grated on him to see his mistakes out in the open, though, and from what he'd heard from his own mouth as he laid his plan out before the beauty beside him, his errors were blaring.

A lifetime of work, down the tube. He'd screwed up, he knew it, and he was certain the Bureau knew it. He'd heard nothing of any investigation as yet, however. With a little luck, maybe there wouldn't be one. *That idiot Tipton had best kept his mouth shut.* The lid on Tipton's death was tighter than a sealed coffin. *Why?*

The Feds knew something. They had to. It irritated him, after all these years of being in control of the flow of information, to now be shut out. As Deputy Director of Research for the National Security Agency, Tristan was made aware of every interesting piece of new technology out there, when it came to national security. Not only access to the technology, he also had sources in every corner and the ability to pay them for information he needed. Now, he knew nothing. His pipeline of information had gone dry, and how much the Feds knew of his 'activities' or how much they didn't know was a mystery to him. He didn't like mysteries.

The Justin Markham fiasco had been handled poorly. Yes, it was a complicated op, and it seemed at every turn it became *more* complicated. However, the sale of Markham's 'fire sale' prevention algorithm would have capped off the fortune Tristan already possessed, ensuring a more than comfortable existence for his remaining days.

He shouldn't have trusted Tipton, should've known he'd make a mess of the whole affair. Now Justin Markham was running around out there with a new face, a new name and a new life, supposedly, and Tristan had nothing. He had less than nothing. How in the world had his life gotten this messed up, anyway?

Tristan examined the marks on the neck of the woman beside him as he picked up his phone from the nightstand and dialed the number of his cleaner. His evening's companion had been lovely, everything he'd wanted her to be. Killing her had been regrettably necessary, for the simple reason if they're dead they don't tell. Anything.

The phone on the other end was ringing.

"Yeah."

"Room 548. The Grand. Body disposal, evidence removal. Sanitize. Money will be under her pillow. I'll be out of the room in forty-five minutes. Room key will be in the usual place."

"Done."

The call ended. He rose from the bed and went into the bathroom, grabbing clean clothes on the way. As he stepped into the shower, his mind wandered back to his early days with the NSA. He'd been straight as an arrow, until the day one William Grantham approached him with a proposal. He'd always respected Bill Grantham, actually wanted to pattern his career after him, and in the beginning he'd been flattered by the trust Grantham placed in him for these 'special' assignments. By the time Tristan figured out what the man was *really* up to, not only was Tristan also deeply involved in illegal activities. He was hooked on the highs that came with it, the money, the lies, the promised lifestyle.

Grantham, now in prison for murder and treason, had been with the Bureau at the time and needed a contact at the NSA he felt he could rely on. He invited Tristan to be a 'delivery boy' for everything from envelopes to packages. Opening anything given him would mean his death; and Grantham had made that part very clear. For each delivery, he was paid five hundred dollars.

As time went on, Grantham's requests became more specific, more…illegal…and his payments had increased substantially. Tristan remembered exactly when he'd realized there was no backing out. Not that he'd wanted to, but in retrospect, he definitely should have. Instead, he watched and he learned how the 'business' was run. He paid special attention to where Grantham's lists of sources was kept, who was in the know and who wasn't.

When Grantham was arrested, Tristan felt it was not just his right , but his responsibility to pick up the man's illegal affairs and take the profits from them himself. At first he was concerned Grantham's trail would lead to Tristan but after a few months of sweating and wondering, everything calmed back down and it was business as usual.

Tristan had millions tucked away in off-shore accounts. He could have retired years ago, but he'd become addicted to the thrill of espionage, the electrifying effect of watching secrets and money change hands, the covert meetings and whispered plans.

Tristan couldn't even use his money in the States. If he lived beyond the income afforded him by his position at the NSA, he'd arouse suspicion and it would all be over. So he'd waited, patiently, deciding at one point he'd retire and move out of the country. Then Justin Markham showed up, and Tristan saw the opportunity for the score of a lifetime. Markham's magic algorithm was to be his last deal, his last big sale. He'd had no idea how true that would be.

The sale never happened; Markham couldn't even remember how to tie his own shoes after Tipton was done with him. Tristan was certain the priceless encryption code, now locked in the head of Neo Weston, would never see the light of day. It was gone, thanks to the misuse of the serum they'd injected him with.

Tristan's initial involvement happened because Markham talked about *giving* the code away! Making it available to every business and household in the world. What was he thinking? There were obscene amounts of money to be made with that code. Markham had no business head whatsoever. Now no one would have that goldmine. It still irritated him to think of it.

He turned off the shower, dried and dressed and returned to the bed. He sat down beside the body of his paid escort. Now the question was how to get rid of the body. He shouldn't have used his credit card to order her 'services.' Bad call. There'd been a lot of those lately. He didn't know if they were tracking him yet, or if he'd even been included in their list of suspects. It all depended on what Tipton told them, and no one was privy to that information.

It shouldn't matter if the FBI found her in his room or not. But why should he hand them evidence on a platter? Tristan was glad he'd called the cleaner and looked forward to his upcoming flight.

He was heading out of the country, happy to be rid of the responsibilities of keeping so much hidden. Now, his life would be ever so much easier. He could come and go as he pleased and live a life of privilege. He'd been thinking about where he wanted to live. With the amount of money he now possessed, he could live anywhere. He could have homes in several different countries. Spain was nice, or so he'd heard. And he liked Italy, although, the German countryside was supposed to be lovely as well. Just so many options it made him smile.

Tristan stood and grabbed his coat, briefcase and roll bag. He could wait at the airport, hidden in the first class lounge, until boarding. Though he'd not planned for it all to end this way, he was happy to be free of the NSA. With one last glance around the room to be sure he'd not left anything, he opened the door and left, placing the 'Do Not Disturb' sign on the knob and closing the door behind him. He slipped the key just under the door where it couldn't be seen, but could easily be slid out if it's position was known.

Tristan stepped off the elevator and saw a group of six FBI agents at the front desk. He took a smooth but quick left turn into the lounge and pulled out his cell phone.

"Yeah."

"Are you in the room?"

"Yes."

"Get out now. Forget about sanitizing, just get the girl out now. Take the service elevator and go out the back way. There are agents in the lobby on their way up to you within the next few minutes. Go. Now."

He'd recognized Cayman Richards and Neo Weston immediately upon exiting the elevator. He'd seen the other four around, as well, but never spoken to them nor had any interaction with them. Tristan peered around the corner into the lobby and watched as Cayman, obviously the leader, spoke to the clerk and nodded, showing his badge before the clerk gave him a room key. He was certain the key was to his room. How could they have found his trail so quickly?

He ducked back to avoid detection. The men entered the elevator and disappeared behind the closing doors. Tristan hurried out the front door and hailed a taxi. Winter was setting in and the rain and snow mix poured from the sky.

"Dulles, please. Make it fast and I'll pay you double." He wiped the water from his shoulders and from the front of his coat, then shook the water from his hat onto the seat beside him.

"Yes, sir!" The taxi sped away from the curb and blended into traffic. Tristan watched the hotel disappear in the side mirror. *That was a close one.*

Tristan wondered if the FBI would be watching the airports. He hadn't thought of that until now. *That's not very professional of me, I should be thinking ahead better than this.* He never had to worry about who was watching what, he'd had people to do that. Now he was on his own. Still, he'd not done too badly, he had his passport ready, fake name, fake ID, if he kept his head down, it was quite possible he'd make it out of this without any problems. Knowing Cayman Richards--that was a really big 'if.'

Picking up his cell phone once more, he auto-dialed one more number.

"It's me, I'm on my way to the airport. You have my flight information, check for the gate. Be ready. You won't have a lot of time."

Tristan hung up the phone and allowed himself to relax…a little. Everything was in place. *If the cleaner didn't make it out of the room in time that's his problem. And who cares if Cayman's little team finds the body. I'm out of here anyway.*

Checking his luggage at the curb, Tristan hurried into the airport, his eyes watching every corner. He couldn't keep looking over his shoulder, as that would make him look suspicious, so he hurried through the security check and went directly to the first class lounge. He'd traveled enough from this airport, he knew exactly where it was.

Once inside the lounge, he found a quiet corner and pulled a newspaper from the seat beside him, burying himself behind it, peeking out every so often to check new arrivals. The lounge was relatively full, which helped his cause quite well. It was easier to hide when you weren't the only person in the room.

From the corner of his eye, Tristan saw the clerk at the desk peer around the corner at him and, once eye contact was made, immediately disappeared. That was his cue to leave.

He slowly folded the newspaper and lay it beside him on the seat. He rose casually and sauntered slowly through the lounge and out the door. Looking back, he saw the lounge attendant pick up the phone. He'd been recognized.

Eventually, Tristan headed to his gate, hiding under his hat and keeping his overcoat on. He arrived at the gate just as the plane was boarding and entered without any issues. Once he set his foot on the passenger boarding bridge, he looked to the end of the bridge and saw his man in charge of 'plan B' waiting right where he said he'd be. Plan B was a go.

Chapter Two

Earlier that morning, Cayman and Neo received word one of Bradford's aliases was used at a downtown D.C. hotel. The information they'd retrieved from Tipton's safe included a list of names used by Bradford on a regular basis. In spite of what Tipton had done, Neo was grateful to him for giving them the contents of his safe before killing himself with the cyanide pill. The information they'd been given proved invaluable in their hunt.

Cayman quickly assembled a team of four agents, Jay Green, Andre Winston, Van Bingham and Preston Glenn they hurried to the hotel. Neo was initially going to lead his own team, but due to the attempted abduction, Cayman opted to keep Neo with him. Neo was fine with the arrangement, as long as it meant he didn't have to sit behind a desk at the Hoover Building while everyone else was hunting the bad guys.

"My name is Cayman Richards," he said, showing the clerk his badge. "I'm a Special Agent with the FBI and I'm looking for this man." Cayman held up a picture of Bradford. "He may have registered under the name of Jamison Stone."

The clerk inspected the badge. He checked the readout on his computer and nodded his head. "We have a Jamison Stone registered. He came in last night with a female companion."

He readied a key card for the appropriate room and handed it to Cayman. "He's on the fifth floor, room 548."

"Thank-you for your cooperation. I'm going to need a master pass key for each of my men. We may need to enter other rooms in our search."

The clerk, his hands now shaking slightly, nodded silently and quickly prepared six master pass key cards. Cayman took the cards and handed them to his team. The men proceeded to the elevators and up to the fifth floor.

The team members cleared the fifth floor of all guests while Neo and Cayman went to Bradford's room. There were only four other rooms occupied on the fifth floor. Once the guests were on the elevator and on their way down to the main floor, the team met up with Cayman and Neo at the door to Bradford's room. Each man drew his gun.

Using the key given him at the front desk, Cayman opened the door and all six men went inside, some to the left and some to the right. The room was quickly assessed and cleared.

"Bingham, you and Glenn sweep the rooms above this floor. He's probably gone, but someone could have tipped him off and he may still be in the hotel. Green, I want you and Winston to sweep the floors below this one. Neo and I will head back down to the lobby and see if Bradford parked a car there. If not, we'll check for taxis that have been here this morning. We'll have to narrow down the fares and see if we can find which one picked up Bradford and where they took him."

The men nodded and were off.

Cayman called to Bingham as they headed to the elevators. "Bingham, when you're done here, text me and find out where I am. We'll plan to meet up wherever the taxi dropped Bradford, assuming he's not still in the hotel. I'm willing to bet it was an airport. If he knows we're onto him, and from the look of it he does, he's going to be trying to get out of the country as fast as he can."

Neo and Cayman checked back at the front desk to see if Bradford had a car parked in the hotel parking garage. There was none. They spoke to the doorman on the way out who'd called for several taxis already this morning, but only had one gentleman walk to the curb and hail a taxi on his own. He had no idea where the gentleman was headed.

"Reagan or Dulles?" Cayman was buckling into his seat.

"I'm betting on Dulles. There are more international flights from there."

Cayman nodded and started the car. "Dulles it is."

Neo turned to Cayman, trying to find an outlet for his frustration. "Where do you think he'll head?"

"Hard to say," replied Cayman. "I'm betting on a country that doesn't have an extradition treaty with the U.S., probably Russia or China."

"You know, Cayman, just when I think I've about got this whole thing behind me, it seems like there's a crick in the plan and everything goes south. I just want my life back, you know? I want this over, I want to enjoy my wife's pregnancy, be there to help her tie her shoes when she can't see her feet."

"I know. I keep saying it's almost over, and really, Neo, when you think of it in terms of your abduction, it *is* almost over. We've only been on this for a few months now, and look how far we've come. Desmond did his best, and he definitely got us pointed in the right direction. We've got this, Neo. We do. Just hang in there with me for a little longer."

"I know, I will. It's just with the baby coming, I feel like I need to speed this up so I don't miss the whole thing."

"She's what, two months along?"

"Yeah, about that."

"We've got time. All you'd be doing right now is rubbing her back while she's bent over the toilet puking. You've got time before the fun stuff begins."

"Yeah, I suppose. I'm just frustrated."

Cayman parked the SUV and the two men strode quickly into the terminal. It was a lot to cover with only two of them, but Neo made a suggestion for a shortcut.

"He'll most likely travel first class, yes?"

"Probably, but that seems pretty stupid…much easier to find."

"Yes," agreed Neo, "and maybe he's stupid…we should check the first class lounges. There can't be *that* many of them. Or we could split up." Neo's dark eyes were focused and determined. He scanned the crowd constantly, checking for that one familiar face.

"I don't think so," said Cayman, busting out his boyish grin. "We should stay together. I need you to protect me."

"Yeah, right. Ya big weenie."

Just then Cayman's text chime went off. It was Bingham. They were on their way, having cleared the hotel and not found Bradford. Cayman and Neo agreed to meet them at the main entrance.

While they waited, Cayman took the photo of Bradford to the nearest ticket agent and asked them to fax it to every first class lounge in the terminal. He gave instructions for anyone who saw Bradford *not* to approach him, but to call Cayman. He left his cell number with the ticket agent, then excused himself and hurried to the main entrance.

Andre Winston was the first one from the SUV and into the terminal. A little breathless, his eyes scanned the terminal until he found Cayman and Neo. He jogged to them and began, "He's on a flight to China, leaving in about twelve minutes. We called ahead and found the reservation, on the off chance he was using the same alias for his flight that he used at the hotel. We also requested they hold the flight."

"Good job. Let's get to the gate."

They ran through the airport, fearful that once the flight was delayed Bradford would bolt and they'd miss him. The team arrived at the gate as the plane was just taking off. Cayman ran to the check-in desk. He held up his badge for the woman at the gate to see.

"Cayman Richards, FBI," he said, breathlessly. "Is that the plane to China?" he gestured out the window. "We asked you to hold it for us, we suspect there is a criminal on board. We need it to return to the terminal immediately."

"I'm truly sorry, sir. We didn't get a message to stop the plane. Let me just call and have them let the tower know to turn the plane around."

The words had no more than left her mouth when there was a huge explosion on the passenger boarding bridge. The windows to the waiting area were blown into the building as part of the wall collapsed onto the floor. The ceiling sagged dangerously over the injured lying beneath it.

Cayman, Neo and their team were protected by the check-in desk and ducked below it, avoiding the flying glass. When they stood, the carnage before them was gut wrenching. A mother with a large piece of glass protruding from her back covered the body of her terrified infant with her own. The wounded lay everywhere, bleeding and bruised.

Neo rushed to the mother and child. Both were still alive, and he left the piece of glass where it was. Easing the screaming child from under his mother's body, he held the baby close to him.

"My...son...please, help...my son."

Neo inspected the baby and found him to be unhurt. "Your baby is uninjured, ma'am. However, you need to lie perfectly still until we can get an EMT for you. Do you understand?"

"Yes...hurts...back hurts."

"You're going to be fine. I'll stay here with you. I have your son."

Neo could only rock the terrified infant and pray he wasn't lying to his mother. The glass fragment was the size of a dinner plate. It went far enough into her skin to stand on it's own, and Neo had no way of knowing how deep that was and what it meant for her internal organs. After what seemed to Neo to be an eternity, the child stopped crying and slept peacefully in his arms. He couldn't stop staring at this little human being, so unaware of what his mother had just done for him. This was a frightening world for children and holding this beautiful little one made him wonder how he could bring another life into it.

Sirens sounded around the outside of the smoke and debris filled waiting area. The room looked like a war zone with upturned chairs and pieces of glass, ceiling, chairs and rails strewn everywhere. People cried out for help, children, terrified and panicked cried and screamed for their parents. Soon EMT's with gurneys ran into the large room. Neo flagged them over and handed them the child. "Ma'am, I have to go help others now, the EMT's have your son. They're going to take care of both of you."

"Thank...you."

Neo rushed over to where Cayman was working with several wounded. "I need pressure on the wound over there," he said, pointing to a man several feet from him.

"I'm on it." Neo hurried to the man. He was bleeding badly from a cut on his shoulder. "Sir, my name is Neo. I'm going to have to put pressure on this wound and it's going to hurt. Hang in there with me." The man barely had the strength to cry out when Neo pressed firmly on the wound. "I'm sorry. The EMT's are here. They'll help you soon."

More EMT's arrived with more gurneys and wounded were loaded into waiting ambulances as quickly as they arrived. Those who could walk were helped out to ride to the hospital with the more seriously wounded. Within an hour the room was cleared of the wounded. There were no fatalities, yet, and for that Neo was grateful.

The team met in the hallway once all the emergency personnel had left with their patients. Crime scene tape had been placed over the entrance to the concourse. CSI had been called along with the FBI bomb squad and the team waited at the concourse entrance until they arrived to ensure no one entered the area.

The plane was never called to return to the gate with all the chaos surrounding the event. Neo knew who planted the bomb and why. They would hunt Bradford down and find him wherever he'd gone. He wouldn't be able to run from this one.

Chapter Three

Adrian Newberg's phone rang, interrupting his afternoon 'meeting.'

"I told you *never* to call me at work. I'm busy. I'm *very* busy."

"I know, Adrian, but the baby's sick and I need to get him to the doctor. I have an appointment in an hour."

"I make good money so you can have a car and then you run it out of gas and expect me to drop everything when you can't get to an appointment. You're going to have to figure something out. I'm sick of your whining."

"Adrian, I *told* you I needed gas. You wouldn't give me any money to *get* gas. You were supposed to give me the money for groceries and gas two nights ago. Then you tell me last night there isn't any. What are we supposed to eat? How am I supposed to get Jake to the doctor? You're going to have to come home."

"Don't tell me what I have to do. *You* take care of the sick kid. Call your stupid neighbor or something, but leave me *alone!*"

Adrian ended the call and rolled back over, once again facing the escort he'd just paid. Although ready to extend their 'meeting' and pay her again, she was out of bed and nearly dressed.

"Get back in bed, I'm not done with you yet."

"You know," she said, continuing to dress, "I'm really surprised you're married." The woman began putting her shoes on.

"Why's that?" Adrian sneered at her, his demeanor still demanding her return to bed.

The woman stood, walked to the side of the bed, and looked down on Adrian with furious cat eyes.

"Because you suck as a human being and you're lousy in bed."

The woman walked to the door, looked over her shoulder and smirked at the man in the bed. She chose her johns, and this one was not a john she'd choose again. She turned the knob and walked out the door, leaving it open just enough that he would have to get up and close it.

Muttering under his breath, he got out of bed and shut the door, grabbed his clothes and went into the bathroom. In an hour he was in his home, standing in an empty house. The furniture was still there, but all of his wife's clothing and belongings were gone, along with their son Jake, and all of his things. She'd left no note and had somehow gotten gas in the car, because her car was gone, as well.

A fine thank you for all I've done for her. She was useless anyway; a complete waste of time, and all that kid ever did was cry. She'll be back as soon as she needs another tank of gas. Then she'll find out just how useless she is.

Adrian held the job of Machine Room Coordinator at the NSA. When he'd received the promotion he was called into Tristan Bradford's office and another offer was made 'under the table.' He would be part of a top secret operation to secure an asset who could change the face of the computer world and make all involved in the op very rich men. He was happy to accept the promotion *and* his inclusion in the operation. It only confirmed in his mind how very valuable *he* was to the NSA. He knew he was invaluable, but it had taken a little longer for his superiors to see his full worth. Now that they'd seen it, and rewarded him with this new op, he'd really show them what he was made of.

At least, that's how he felt in the beginning. Now, with Wesley Tipton dead and Tristan Bradford seemingly MIA, all communications were suddenly closed up and nobody was talking. Something was wrong and Adrian knew it. The big question for him was, after all the work he'd done, setting up private, encrypted computer files to store all their communiqués, monitoring computer usage by the team, making sure everything stayed under the radar, all the risks he'd taken…was he going to get paid? He'd better. He'd really put himself out on a limb for this op. *Really* out on a limb. He was sure no one had sacrificed to the extent he had.

The fact that no one had heard from Tristan Bradford for days made Adrian very uncomfortable. He couldn't help but wonder if everyone was on the run. Fairly sure no one could link him to any of the rogue activities; his mind reviewed his impeccable service record. He was certain if he wanted to, he could get into the academy and become an agent now that he didn't have a wife and kid chained to his ankle. He just might do that.

Adrian's phone rang and he picked it up. "You better get out of the country fast. I don't know what Tipton said, but Bradford's gone missing and I bet they'll start picking us off one by one. Who knows…maybe *they* have Bradford and they're keeping it under wraps." The caller was Raymond Mathens, one of the leaders of the rogue op and his direct superior in that operation.

"What do you mean? How could they be onto *all* of us?"

"Had to be Tipton. He was such a weasel. Probably ratted us out and then they killed him."

"Are you leaving? What about your family? Where will you go?"

"Well, that's the thing. I don't really have a family."

"You *what*?"

"I said, I don't really have a family. I made them all up. I needed people to think I was a family guy, you know? When you tell another woman who's looking for some… 'understanding,' you get a lot further with her if you're married. She knows you understand where she's been, what she's going through."

Adrian couldn't believe what he was hearing. How do you make up a whole family? "Whatever. Where are you going?"

"I'm headed to Brazil. Lots of places to hide there, beautiful places, leaving tonight."

"How are you paying for that?"

The call ended suddenly and Adrian knew he'd been duped. Had everyone been paid but him? How did they get their money?

His face grew red with rage. His fists were clenched at his side, the car keys in his hand breaking into the skin of his palm. He screamed in frustration, no words, just a hideous, pathetic scream as the blood dripped from his palm.

***

Cayman's team continued checking the airport for signs of Bradford. He and Neo were leaving gate when Cayman stopped, mid-stride.

"What's wrong?" Neo studied his friend's face.

Cayman ran his hands through his hair and started for the main check-in counters.

"Where are you going?"

"I'm following up on a hunch that's been nagging me since the explosion." They walked to the airline counter and, after showing the clerk their ID Cayman asked to have a passenger check of every passenger on board the aircraft that left just prior to the explosion.

"That will take a few minutes. We'll have to radio the aircraft from the tower."

"I can wait."

The clerk picked up his phone and made the call. Cayman and Neo waited off to the side of the line of people.

"What if Bradford never got on that airplane? What if the explosion was a ruse set up to allow him ample time to get away? What if Bradford is still in the States?"

Neo's eyes widened. "Or…what if he had tickets for two planes, or three, or four and knew we'd be checking this one because he used the same name as he did at the hotel? What if he's leaving the country on another airline? Heading to another destination, using a different ID for each destination?"

Cayman pulled out his cell phone, his eyes angry and determined. "Jennifer, I want you to go into my office and find the sheet with the list of Tristan Bradford's aliases on my desk. Get as much help as you need with this, and make it top priority. I need you to distribute those names to every airline, both large and small, within a one hundred mile radius of D.C. airports. Find out if Bradford booked a flight to anywhere, how many, and which names actually had a checked in for the flight and walked down that jet bridge. Also check bus and train stations. Send instructions to the TSA that anyone checking in for a flight under any of those aliases is to be detained and they're to notify me immediately. I want confirmation the job is done ASAP."

He ended the call and saw the clerk at the desk flagging him over.

"Sir, there was one passenger on the manifest that actually checked in for the flight, but never boarded. It was this one." The clerk pointed to the name Jamison Stone on the passenger manifest.

"*Idiot!* How could I have been so stupid! I assumed because he'd checked in at the gate, he'd actually boarded the plane. He sent us on a wild goose chase and I swallowed his bait without even thinking it through."

"We all did, Cayman, don't beat yourself up. We all did the same thing." Neo was gritting his teeth. "He's going to be long gone by now anyway."

Cayman took the manifest from the clerk and scanned the area for his team. Pulling his two-way from the belt clip, he called the team. "Team members return to the main terminal. Return to the main terminal. Please acknowledge."

Each team member responded and within minutes they joined Neo and Cayman.

"It looks like Bradford may have played us and never got *on* that plane. We need to get back to the office. We'll meet you back there."

Neo and Cayman found their SUV and headed out.

"This was a fiasco. I better have some answers when I get back to the office or heads will roll."

"Don't take your frustration out on the staff. I'm sure they're doing the best they can. This is the level of frustration I've become accustomed to, Cayman. Just take deep breaths and calm yourself. Letting the frustration get the best of you is only going to reduce your ability to think rationally."

"You sound like a sniper."

"I *am* a sniper."

Chapter Four

At the airport, Adrian lined up to board the plane. He was flying first class for the first time in his life. The money he'd stashed in the bank vault had come in very handy. It was Bradford who told him to stash the money, and he was glad he'd followed that advice. It would get him out of the country and hopefully set up comfortably in Mexico. He'd heard you could live pretty cheaply down there. Who would look for him there? *In fact*, he wondered to himself with an overconfident smile, *who would know to even look for him at all?*

He buckled in and rubbed his hands over the fine leather seat as a man in a suit approached. Adrian's smile faded. He knew those kinds of suits.

"Mr. Adrian Newberg, I need to ask you to come with me, please."

Adrian went instantly pale. "Why? Who are you? What do you want with me?"

The agent displayed his badge, identifying himself as an FBI agent. "I need you to come with me quietly."

Adrian's knees where shaking so badly he wasn't sure he'd be able to stand. He managed somehow, and was escorted off the plane. Once back in the terminal he was placed in handcuffs right there for all to see, his rights were read to him and he was taken to the Hoover building for questioning. He was led to an interrogation room and chained to a chair.

Neo watched him from the observation room. "I want this one, Cayman. I'm ready to do some interrogating, I believe I'm ready."

"Okay, he's all yours then, but I want you to take a minute and go to the conference room for me first."

"What? Go where?"

"You heard me. I want you to go to the conference room. Spend a minute there, gather your thoughts and then come back here when you're ready."

"What is this? Am I back in kindergarten? I *can* effectively interrogate a suspect, you know. I've done it dozens of times."

"Neo, would you humor me and go take a couple minutes in the conference room? Please? I just need to know that your head is where it needs to be, that you're not going to lose it in there. Take a few minutes, go through the motions of an interrogation in your head and see how you feel about it. You're pretty emotionally tied to this investigation and you need to be sure you can be objective."

Neo sighed and lifted his arms helplessly, letting them fall loosely back down to his side. Shrugging his shoulders, he left observation and headed to the conference room, muttering to himself the whole way.

"What in the world? Am I a child? I have to go think about what I want to say? This is so ridic--"

He opened the conference room door, not noticing the guard stationed outside the room. As soon as he opened the door he saw her, and the guard said softly, "Please step inside quickly, Mr. Weston." He did, trying not to stumble over his own feet, and the guard shut the door behind him.

A smile exploded across the surface of Sophia's face as she ran to him and threw herself on him, wrapping both arms around him and sobbing. He set her down, the beating of his heart so loud he could hardly hear her sobs. He took her face in his hands, not knowing where to start, what to say.

"Is it really you? Am I dreaming?" He kissed her lips, feeling their warmth, and molded himself around her, holding her so tightly he could feel her heart beating against his chest. "Sophia, Sophia...how did you get here? Never mind. I really don't care how, I'm just so happy to see you."

"Neo," she said, whispering in his ear, "I never thought this day would come. I love you, Neo, I never want to leave you again."

He stopped breathing, pulled her from him and stared in awe at her. "What do you mean? What are you saying? You're back to stay? You're here for good?"

Sophia's eyes filled with tears. "I never left," she said giggling. "I've been hidden away here in D.C., both myself and Mrs. Barbosa. We couldn't tell you. Keeping that secret was the hardest thing I've ever done. We have a penthouse suite on the top floor of an apartment complex. It's beautiful, and the only thing it's been missing is you."

Suddenly Neo remembered Sophia was carrying their child. His eyes widened and he placed her at arm's length and scanned her belly. Kneeling in front of her, he laid his head softly on her stomach and listened. Sophia held his head, gently pressing it against her, loving how much he already loved their child. It brought tears to her eyes, and a small sob escaped her lips.

"I'm going to help you tie your shoes," he whispered.

Sophia giggled. "I don't think she'll be needing that for a while, my love."

Neo stood and hugged her. "Not the baby, I'm going to help *you* tie your shoes when you can't see your feet. I'm going to be right there, helping you. And…did you say *she*?"

Sophia laughed through her tears. "Well, it's better than 'it' don't you think? And you said 'she' too, you know."

"I did say that, didn't I? I don't care which it is. I'm so in love with you I can't see straight. I knew I'd missed you, but not exactly how much until I saw you standing here. You are my world, Sophia. My life, you're every breath I take in and send out. You have captured my soul, and I give it to you willingly."

Cayman knocked softly on the door and walked in. "Hope I'm not interrupting anything."

Neo stuck his hand out and shook Cayman's. "Thank you." His face grew serious and he continued. "Are you sure it's safe for her to be here? For us to be together?"

"We're going to have guards stationed outside your penthouse every day until we know everyone is accounted for. The leaders of the rogue operation are leaving the country en masse and I believe the worker bees beneath them are also all accounted for. We have a lot of work to do, yet, Neo, but I thought maybe you'd be a little easier to live with if you were aware your wife was just down the block."

"That was just mean, you know," he said, referring to Cayman's suggestion to 'gather his thoughts' in the conference room. Neo gazed softly into the beautiful deep blue eyes of his wife. Her hair seemed more blonde, her eyes more blue. "But you're forgiven."

"That's good to know. I wasn't sure what I was going to do for a minute there. It's never good to have a sniper upset with you."

Neo smiled and kissed Sophia one more time. "I've gotta go interrogate a suspect. I'll be home for dinner, Mrs. Weston, as soon as I find out where I live."

Sophia laughed. "I'll be expecting you."

Sam and Patrick strolled into the room, grinning widely. "We'll be taking the little lady home now, sir."

"*You?* You've been her bodyguards this whole time?"

Sam spoke up first. "That's right. You can thank us later with a nice thick steak dinner and as much beer as we can legally swallow in one night." Sam's dark eyes and hair made Neo do a double-take. Sam looked to his fair-haired brother for acknowledgement. "Right?"

"Exactly," agreed Patrick.

Neo looked at Patrick and Cayman. "You're sure he's not adopted?"

"No, not adopted," chuckled Cayman, "but Dad teased Mom about the milk man for *years.*"

Neo's eyes bored into Sam's. "I'll bet every girl you ever dated was jealous of those eyelashes. I forgot about those things. You could trim them halfway in and you'd still have plenty. You've got girlie eyes, Sam, pure and simple...they're girlie eyes."

"Yes, as I'm frequently reminded by my warm and caring brothers. However, my wife, Jada, points out that our daughter has my eyelashes, and how she will thank me for the rest of her life."

Smiling, Neo stared down at the love of his life. "Thanks for keeping her safe." He released her reluctantly and she left the room with a Richards boy on either side of her.

Neo punched Cayman playfully on the arm. "Why didn't you tell me she was in here?"

"Just trying to keep the people in the hallways safe from you burning rubber all the way from observation. We wouldn't want to be paying out workers' comp to all of them, now would we?"

"Cute. Let's go get ourselves a bad guy. I'm really in the mood for some 'interrogatin.'"

Cayman laughed and clapped him on the back. Together they went into the interrogation room where Adrian Newberg sat not so patiently waiting for them.

"Mr. Newberg," began Neo, "we have information that tells us you are part of a rogue team of agents responsible for the death of one..." he opened the file on the table before him. "...Justin Markham, is that right?"

"I...I'm not responsible for anyone's death. No one died in our op, we only made people think the Markham kid died." The blood was draining quickly from Adrian's face.

"No one died? Not one person?"

"Not one person. We were very careful."

"What about that 'Markham kid's' family? Were they not counted as people in the eyes of your operation?"

"I don't know anything about that. His family died? No one said anything to me about that. I'm not taking the wrap for murder. That wasn't what I signed up for."

"I see." Neo was maintaining his calm demeanor rather well. "Do you know who I am?"

"No, I don't. Should I?"

"Yes, you should. You helped create me."

"I don't understand." Adrian was studying Neo's face.

"My name used to be Justin Markham. I'm now known as Neo Weston. My facial features were changed, my family was killed so their financial assets could be used to fund your operation and I was made to believe I was someone else for more than twelve months. Is that ringing any bells?"

Adrian's eyes widened.

"Yeah, I can see it's beginning to register. Well, while you're digesting that, my mother, my father and my brother were *all* people to me. They were *more* than people to me…they were family. And yes, my unlucky little man, you *will* pay for their deaths, for you are guilty by association, and I'll see you in court."

Neo rose and walked to the door with Cayman behind him. Adrian screamed as they left. "I want a deal! I'll tell you everything I know. I want a deal!"

The two interrogators continued to the door and exited the room.

"*That* was incredibly satisfying," smiled Neo. "Let's let him stew in a cell for a while. Maybe he'll remember some things to make his 'deal' more appealing to us." Neo scanned the hallway for a moment, then continued. "I'm going home, as soon as you can take me. Apparently I don't know where I live."

Cayman smiled. "Happy to assist. We'll get an SUV assigned to you by tomorrow so you'll have some wheels. I'll pick you up in the morning. And just so we're clear, I'm not sending anyone to go get you; no one has been or will be asked to do this for me. *I'll* be the one picking you up. Got it?"

"Got it. I'm beat, going to get some sleep tonight, no doubt."

Cayman started laughing. "*Sure* you are. Do you know who you're talking to here? Yeah, if you get ten minutes of sleep tonight, I'll eat my shoes tomorrow morning."

"Whoa. That sounds like a bet and I'll take it. You're going to be chewing some leather tomorrow."

Cayman shook his head with a hopeless grin as the two men left his office.

Chapter Five

Having Sophia's arms around his neck and her lips on his was the most wonderful feeling in the world. He could've stayed right there in the entryway all night, never moving from that spot. He loved how her belly was beginning to swell, such a tiny amount that he was the only one who would notice, besides Sophia herself. He couldn't wait to feel their child move and kick inside her.

Suddenly the reverie was broken by the strong accent and boisterous voice of Mrs. Barbosa. "You going to eat what I cook or kiss-kiss like lovesick birds?"

Neo chuckled and stared down into the beautiful face of his wife. "We're going to stand here like-"

"Oh no you not!" Mrs. Barbosa's voice was louder with each word. "I get a hose if I need. You eat my dinner before it cold. I got a new broom, Mr. Neo. I not afraid to use it."

Neo laughed and he and Sophia walked arm-in-arm into the living room. The penthouse was beautiful with windows reaching from the floor to the ceiling across the dining room and extending into the living room. The space was open and expansive, making you feel as if you were flying over the city.

"I like it," he said, sitting down at the large oak table and scanning his new home. "I like it a lot. Did you two pick out this furniture? It's perfect."

"Yes, we did," replied Sophia, glowing at the cook. "Mrs. Barbosa has quite an eye for shapes and colors. I think she did most of the finding. She's amazing."

Mrs. Barbosa sat down at the table, nodding respectfully to Neo and Sophia, obviously proud of her work.

"How did you ever talk her into joining us at the table? I've been trying to do that for years." Neo was surprised to see her sitting comfortably with them and not complaining about it.

"She use blackmail," scowled Mrs. Barbosa. "Mrs. Neo tell me if I no eat at table, she will help in kitchen. I have no choice."

Neo laughed. "Now, why didn't I think of doing that?"

"Because you're a man," teased Sophia.

The family ate their dinner, talking about life 'on the run' and what they'd learned from all of it. However, when it came to discussing their abduction, Sophia became very quiet.

"I can't talk about this," she said softly. "I…I just can't."

Neo reached over and took her hand. "Do you need to talk to someone? We can get you some help with that, you know."

"I…I know," she smiled weakly. "It's just…I didn't know how to protect Mrs. Barbosa or myself. I felt sick all the time and thought it was nerves; I was worried about you, scared of making the wrong decision about where to stay and how to remain hidden. I…I felt powerless. There, I said it. I felt powerless to protect us and I never want to feel that way again."

"You'll never have to. I'm going to protect you, with everything I have. I promise you both that. And once our baby is born, we're going to take some self-defense classes together. I want to take care of you, but I need to know when I'm not here you can take care of yourself." He nodded to Sophia and Mrs. Barbosa. Then sliding off his chair and kneeling beside Sophia, he patted her stomach softly, and said, "I promise I'll do my best to take care of all three of you."

Sophia lifted his hand and held it to her cheek. "I know you will."

Mrs. Barbosa was dabbing her eyes with her napkin. "If you don't eat my food I no cook for you tomorrow night. I mean it. Eat your dinner."

Neo returned to his chair, still wondering if he should look into having Leon come by and visit with Sophia. He'd have to think on that. He should have known she'd have residual issues with her abduction. He kicked himself for not paying attention to that.

Sophia's morning sickness was happening at night, and what she ate for dinner came up immediately after she'd put her plate in the sink. As she ran for the bathroom, Neo was right behind her and stood beside her with one hand holding her hair out of the way and the other hand on her back, rubbing it slowly, telling her she would be okay.

He thought she'd collapse in his arms after all the retching she did, but she stood up, walked to the sink, splashed some cold water on her face and patted it dry with a towel.

"Much better," she said smiling broadly. "Much better."

Neo stared at her like she'd lost her mind. "You just threw up for at least three minutes solid. You lost every bit of your dinner. How can you say you feel much better? How can you not want to go to bed for a week?"

"I don't know," she replied with a shrug. "I just feel like I can't wait until I throw up, and when I do, I feel so much better. It's way worth the three minutes. I only know what I feel, and I feel much better."

This was just the beginning of a whole new experience for Neo. He could tell there was much to learn about pregnancy, and no matter what, he would learn it.

That night as they got ready for bed, the morning sickness kicked in again, only this time she didn't feel as good after throwing up. She felt bad their first night together she was sick again, but Neo didn't care. Because he was home now, he could hold her in his arms until she fell asleep, stand beside her as many times as she needed to throw up all the while rubbing her back and doing what he could to make her comfortable.

As her breathing steadied and she relaxed into him, he kissed the top of her head. Neo was so happy to be home, so filled with contentment. With Sophia in his arms, together in their own place, he was finally home. As he drifted off to sleep, he couldn't help the smile that spread across his face. Cayman was chewing leather in the morning, and Neo didn't even care.

***

The good part about the sudden exodus of the top leadership of the rogue operation was that none of the 'lower level' leadership were prepared with fake identities, except for those who already possessed them. Rounding them up was happening faster than expected. The one man who continued to elude them was Tristan Bradford. He'd become quite invisible.

Bradford, as suspected, had checked in on several flights, from several different airports in the D.C. area, both large and small. It took hours to find out which one he'd actually boarded, if in fact, he'd boarded any of them. Cayman's staff eventually discovered he appeared to have boarded one and, if it really was Bradford in the assigned seat, he was currently on his way to Italy. By the time the discovery was made his flight was past the point of no return, without sufficient fuel to make the trip back to the airport. There was no way to check his ID without putting the whole flight at risk. It was decided they would have Italian authorities awaiting his arrival at the airport there.

***

Raymond Mathens, supervisor to Desmond Ashler, made his way to the first-class boarding line and proceeded through check-in smoothly. His alias, Matthew Whiting, was holding for now, but he knew how these investigations went and he was skittish. He checked the terminal behind him several times as the boarding was beginning and was confident no one was watching him.

Once on the plane, Mathens buckled in and studied each person as they passed his seat. Forcing himself to relax, he released his white-knuckled grip on the armrests and gazed out the window, breathing deeply. The twenty minutes it took for everyone to board seemed like hours, but finally the doors closed and the flight attendants began their preflight instruction. He was home free.

He wasn't sure what it was going to be like in Brazil, wondered how he would figure out where he wanted to live out his days. It was a large country, with lots of quiet little corners perfect for hiding in. He'd begun a course in Portuguese, barely finishing it prior to everything coming apart at the seams in their organization. He at least had the basics down and that would help him make his way, or so he hoped. He'd also applied for a visa to enter Brazil months ago just in case he needed to leave in a hurry. Now, as he was leaving in a *big* hurry, he was certainly glad he did.

The plane taxied out to the runway and Mathens soon felt the familiar force of gravity as he was pushed back into his seat at takeoff. He watched the city shrink below him then disappear through the clouds. There was just something about flight that made him pensive, and he could feel himself sinking into that place where he thought about his life, his choices and the consequences of those choices.

He'd definitely made a bad career decision by hooking up with Wesley Tipton. What was he thinking back then? The situation with Markham and that whole fiasco was ridiculous. The upper echelons of the rogue operation were constantly changing the rules of the op. There'd never been a plan to kill Markham's family, at least none that he'd ever been made aware of. No one ever discussed that contingency or addressed it in any form. Suddenly he was told the Markhams were dead and their assets were to be used to fund the op under Justin Markham's name. Dead? He'd been stunned. It was all too easy for the leadership to do, and the cover up wasn't even an issue. No one knew for sure the deaths of the family members was anything but an accident, but the sheer convenience of it made that possibility difficult to overlook, at least for Mathens. He should have gotten himself out of there then, but it was impossible to leave an organization like that without being killed. He should have thought this through better. Way better.

Raymond reflected on the 'relationship' he now had with the very missing Tristan Bradford. That relationship would most definitely protect him if his hour of need should ever rear its ugly face. He knew where Tristan's wife was buried.

Margo Bradford went missing nine years ago and Tristan had played the wounded husband perfectly, saying his wife had been threatening to leave him for many years. He admitted to the authorities to wishing she would just 'cut the cord' and get it over with, but tearfully told them he never forced that issue because he knew he couldn't live without her. He thought she couldn't actually bring herself to tell him she was leaving, so she ran. He told them her suitcase set was missing along with many of her clothes and her jewels. They bought it all, filed it as a missing person's case and left it at that.

However, a few years later, Raymond found a note while snooping through piles of paperwork on Tristan's desk. The note was obviously from the person he'd hired for the hit on his wife, and the author was threatening blackmail. There was evidently a fight over how much should have been paid versus how much was *actually* paid, and the shooter was threatening to go dig up the body and deliver it to the authorities, anonymously, of course. In the note, the hit man stated the exact location of Margo Bradford's body. Raymond made a copy of the note for his own 'file' and kept it where no one would ever find it.

Tristan Bradford was a bit obsessive/compulsive and saw Raymond leave his office as he was returning. Raymond gave Tristan some lame excuse about looking for a memo he was missing and needed a copy of. Tristan knew the note had been moved and cursed himself for being stupid enough to hide it on his desk. He'd only just received it at the time and had left immediately for a meeting with his blackmailer, whom he'd promptly killed. Raymond let him know he had a copy of the note and would turn it into the authorities at the first sign of trouble.

Yes, he had insurance, and it had proven worth having. He'd told Tristan he had people who would mail that note to the authorities in the event of his death. Tristan was over a barrel and they both knew it. Raymond was safe, and *he* knew it. It was all so…convenient.

The flight from D.C. to Rio De Janeiro, Brazil, was about fifteen and a half hours; long enough to get some sleep and be ready for the work ahead. He had a lot he needed to accomplish once he got there. Leaving D.C. in the early evening, he would arrive in Rio the next morning, so if he could get some sleep while in the air maybe the jet lag wouldn't be too bad. He'd made reservations at a hotel near the airport where he would stay until he could find a permanent place to live. That might take some travel time in itself.

He'd never been to Brazil before and didn't know where anything was. He'd hire a guide to show him around. That would work the best. Yes, things were looking up. He was about to start a whole new life, and he was happy. After a nice dinner, Raymond put his seat back, covered his eyes with a black sleep mask and fell asleep.

The plane stopped at the gate and each passenger made preparations to disembark. Raymond's feet had no sooner hit the terminal floor when a bullet hit him square between the eyes and he went down amidst screams and shrieks from passengers. Everyone ran for cover, hiding behind seats or anything that would provide at least some cover. But there were no more bullets. There was no shooter. The gun apparently had a suppressor and no one saw where the shot originated nor did they see anyone with a gun. It was over almost the minute it happened. Raymond Mathens was dead.

Chapter Six

As it turned out, Cayman didn't chew any leather that next morning, but smiled appreciatively as Neo told him about Sophia's morning sickness. It seemed for her, it was morning and night sickness, unfortunately.

"You'll just have to endure this for, maybe, another month. Of course, most women are over it by this time in their pregnancy, but some of them have it the whole time they're pregnant. I'm sure that won't be the case with Sophia," Cayman smiled like a fox. "However, the fun doesn't end with the end of morning sickness. Once Sophia's over that, then you're into the cravings. Ice cream at one in the morning, peanut butter and pickle sandwiches with mayonnaise and lettuce, specific candy bars and flavored licorice - "

Neo interrupted. "I hear you. I will prepare myself for living with an alien for the next five months. Nice." He rolled his shoulders back and his face took on a look of firm determination. He took a deep breath and blew it out. "I can do this. I know I can."

Cayman laughed and the two men got down to business.

It was several hours after the flight landed in Brazil that Cayman and Neo received the news of the murder of an American passenger, Matthew Whiting, in the terminal at the airport in Rio De Janeiro. A picture of Bradford was faxed to the airport immediately requesting they check to see if anyone had seen or spoken with him in the terminal. They needed to determine if he was the shooter.

Checking Tipton's information, they knew immediately the name Matthew Whiting was an alias belonging to Raymond Mathens. How had he gotten through security with his name on a list of suspected FBI rogue agents?

The frustration in both Neo and Cayman was apparent.

"Mathens must have had something on someone that made him a loose cannon. Someone wanted to make sure he didn't talk." Cayman leaned back in his chair.

Neo sat across the desk from him, staring at the desktop. "If it was Bradford, then he's in Brazil. Or at least he was. It will be interesting to find out if anyone saw him there. If not, then he must have hired a hit man for the job. In his position at the NSA, he certainly could have had the necessary connections. We'll just have to wait and see how this all pans out."

The two men brainstormed for the next while, trying to imagine how the situation at the airport in Rio could have come down. Nothing seemed to make sense. Tristan Bradford had not been spotted at the airport in Brazil. It was true that just because Bradford wasn't actually *seen* at the airport didn't mean he wasn't there. If he *wasn't* there, it could mean he'd hired someone in Brazil to do his dirty work for him. However, finding someone on the street with the skill it took to hit Mathens in the center of the forehead without being seen was next to impossible. If this was an ordered hit, the shooter was professional all the way.

"He could have a contact down there and gave him a call." Neo was stroking his chin, deep in thought.

"Yes, I suppose so, but right now I don't really care who shot Raymond Mathens. I want Tristan Bradford. I was hoping he was the shooter, and I'm not entirely convinced he wasn't."

Neo leaned back and clasped his hands behind his head. "We now know that two of the ten leaders of the op are dead, Tipton and Mathens. But my curiosity is getting the better of me. I can't help but wonder why Bradford would kill Mathens."

"He's cleaning house. Mathens had to know something that Bradford needed kept quiet."

"Would be nice to know what that was."

There was a knock at Cayman's office door. "Come in."

Jennifer, Cayman's administrative assistant, came in. "You're going to want to see this, I'm guessing," she said, laying an envelope on the desk. "It was delivered anonymously by courier company with verbal instructions to see that it was delivered to you." She laid the envelope on Cayman's desk.

"Thanks, Jennifer." She nodded and left the room, closing the door behind her.

Cayman stared at the writing on the envelope. He opened his desk drawer and pulled out a pair of latex gloves, forcing his hands into them, never taking his eyes off the envelope. Once the gloves were in place, he picked it up, and turned the addressed side toward Neo. "You recognize that handwriting?"

The address was handwritten and the words simply said, "To Whom it May Concern."

"Not particularly. Seems a little familiar, but...no, not anything I can put my finger on."

Cayman broke the seal on the envelope and opened it up. It was a photocopy, seemingly several years old, of a letter to Tristan Bradford, with the specifics of the murder of his wife from someone seeking more money for the completed job. There was no information as to who wrote the note, but it appeared someone else added a chilling threat to the bottom of it. It simply said, "I know your secret." That handwriting was the same as the hand that wrote the words on the outside of the envelope.

"Someone was blackmailing Bradford. Seems Bradford ordered a hit on his wife, definitely a job he wouldn't have done himself. I doubt he'd want to get his hands that dirty. From the look of the note, both the writers could've been blackmailing him. This information is going to be just what we've needed. What we've got here is evidence of murder, and if we can't get him on charges pertaining to our current investigation, we can now get him on murder. I'd be willing to bet this came from Raymond Mathens and *that's* why he was killed. This gives us coordinates to where the body is supposedly buried. Interesting. I'll get someone on it."

Cayman rose and strode to the door. He called out for two agents from his strike team, Winston and Bingham. "Come in here for a minute."

The men nodded and headed to his office, closing the door behind them.

"I want you two to investigate this," he said, handing a copy of the note he'd just received to Winston. "Let me know what you find and where you find it. I want to know what's close to it, buildings, neighborhoods, etc. Get back to me as soon as you have your findings."

"Will do," said Winston, and the two men left.

"I wonder where that came from," Neo was staring at the note, lying once again on Cayman's desk.

"Interesting, isn't it? Talk about housecleaning. When times get tough these rogue groups turn on each other like feeding piranha. I'd bet good money that this has a lot to do with Mathens' death. I'll have it checked for prints and just for fun, I'm going to have the handwriting compared to Mathens' handwriting."

***

Agent Winston pulled up to the coordinates, which happened to be in an upscale subdivision in Bethesda. He radioed the office and had them check the address to see if the home belonged to anyone of interest. He reached down and switched on the flashing lights and they rushed to the site. The call came back over the radio as they drove that the home was currently a bank owned property and previous owners had no ties to the NSA or the FBI.

They pulled into the driveway and exited their vehicle, walking slowly toward the backyard. As the two men approached the back of the house, they could hear the sliding sound of dirt against shovel. They made their way soundlessly around the end of the house. Winston motioned for Agent Bingham to stay low and both men flattened themselves against the house.

Peeking around the corner, Winston saw a hooded man digging in the backyard. As he moved back around, Winston's foot hit a hose bib and the sound of digging stopped abruptly. Pulling his gun, he came back around the end of the house.

"Stop right there."

The man had already pulled his gun and a shot rang out, hitting Winston in the shoulder as he came around the corner of the house. Winston flew back against the side of the house and slid to the ground. Bingham flattened himself against the house and peered carefully around. The man in the hoodie was retreating and Winston was leaning against the house, bleeding from the wound in his shoulder. Taking aim at the now retreating figure, Bingham fired. The man stopped long enough to turn and return fire, but missed his target. He turned back around and continued running.

Bingham rushed to his friend's side and removed his own coat, pressing it against Winston's wound.

"You're going to be okay," he said carefully moving his partner and checking under the wound. "It looks like a through and through."

His hand bloody from holding the coat in place, Bingham quickly pulled his cell phone out and pressed the auto dial for an ambulance. He gave them the code for 'agent down' and coordinates to their location.

Checking the wound, Bingham watched his partner and friend for signs of shock. "Stay with me Andre. Stay with me. Help is on the way."

Winston's voice was breathy and weak. "That…was…Bradford. Call Cayman… *now!*"

Chapter Seven

The call came in that Bradford had been spotted and an agent was down, an ambulance was on the way. Cayman made the call to his team leaders as they rushed from the room and out to the car. "I want teams two and three with me. I'm heading to these coordinates," Cayman read them into the radio. "We've had a sighting of Bradford there. Team two, I want you to split up and cover west of the coordinates. Tell team three I want them to do the same thing on the east. Neo and I will take north and south. Call in the local LEO's and get roadblocks set up and watches at airports, busses, trains and subways. Also, check any private carriers for departures and arrivals; show them Bradford's photo."

Cayman started the siren and lights on his car and they sped to the scene of the shooting. When they arrived on scene, Bingham informed them the ambulance had already taken Agent Winston to the hospital. He said Winston was stable when they put him in the ambulance. Agent Bingham's dark eyes were angry. "Bradford's a coward. He shot him and then took off running. Looks like he never got what he came for, though."

Van Bingham's dark hair never moved. Perfectly combed and sprayed in place he always looked like he'd just come from a haircut. He was just as precise with his job as he was with his dress. He'd been incredibly busy after his call to Cayman. He'd kept his partner from bleeding out by applying pressure to the wound until paramedics arrived, taped off the area as a crime scene and made notes of the encounter, all before Cayman and Neo got there.

"You've done a good job, Agent Bingham. File your report and go home. We have plenty of agents who can stay here and supervise the excavation. Understood?"

Agent Bingham was going to argue the point, but acquiesced. "Understood."

Cayman turned to Neo. "Bradford is in the States. Unless he has a private way in and out of the country, we'll get him. And in case he does, we'll be checking the private carriers as well. He's not getting out of the country again. I want this excavation finished. It may not be evidence in the FBI/NSA investigation, but one way or another, it will land him in prison where he belongs."

Neo stared blankly at Cayman. "What if he knows where Sophia is? What if he tries to take her again?"

"We have guards at your penthouse day and night, Neo. We've set up video equipment and alarms. No one is getting in there."

"Yeah, yeah, I know. It's just that he got into and out of Brazil, into and out of the U.S. It's like he's invisible. It makes me nervous, that's all."

"I hear you. We'll double the guard and set up an extra watch in the entrances into the building and in the lobby."

"Thanks, that helps."

Neo decided he'd be working on an escape plan with Sophia and Mrs. Barbosa as soon as he got home that night.

Cayman put his phone to his ear after dialing CSI. "I need a team at the coordinates I just send you. We have a possible buried body to excavate."

It wasn't until later in the day Cayman received a report from the CSI team. There was a body where the hooded man was digging. Preliminary reports stated it as a female in her forties who'd been buried for several years. Forensics was working on identifying the body, using dental records of Bradford's wife. Having a name to begin their search with would definitely shorten the time it normally took to identify the body in an unmarked grave. In the mean time, the search for Bradford would continue.

The sheer volume of tickets Bradford had purchased, and transport mediums he used when he initially left the country made finding *how* he left the States nearly impossible. There were not just tickets out of D.C., but two other states also had several airports with ticket purchases by one or more of Bradford's aliases. Cayman was sure he'd used a new alias no one was aware of for the flight he actually boarded. None of the known aliases turned up anything, and by the time all of them were thoroughly investigated, Bradford would be long gone, unless the hooded man *was* Bradford. They had no way of knowing for sure. Winston thought it was, but how could he have known for sure? It was dark enough they needed a flashlight to see, Winston was wounded, and certainly couldn't have positively identified his own mother at the time of the shooting. The thought made him grit his teeth. It was going to take weeks to discover where he went, and by the time they figured it out, he would have disappeared into the crowd.

The FBI connected with Interpol, who agreed to keep an eye out for Bradford throughout Europe on the off chance the hooded figure who shot Winston wasn't Bradford. If he was still in the States, both Cayman and Neo were certain he'd be found eventually.

***

Tristan Bradford stepped off the plane in Barcelona, Spain. He'd created enough of a smoke screen in the States he was certain no one would find him. He wasn't staying in Spain, anyway. He had a new identity, one not known by any of his associates, and he had a new life ahead of him. All of his money was stashed in different accounts both in France and Switzerland. He was set. In a few hours he would be on his way to Zurich and no one would ever find him.

Initially he'd considered staying in Barcelona for the night, but something told him he should move on immediately. He always listened to that little voice, and today was going to be no different. He would rent a car, drive to Toulouse and spend the night there. The smell of freedom permeated his nostrils and sent his blood tingling through his veins. He felt alive again, ready to live without always checking over his shoulder. He would never have to do that again, and the thought made him smile.

It was late afternoon when he arrived in Toulouse and after an all-night flight with little to no sleep he should have been ready to crash. But Tristan had things to do. He set his suitcase and bags on the bed, rummaging through his carry-on to find a driver's license he'd lifted from someone in the airport. He pulled out his portable scanner and his small portable laminator, along with his high resolution portable printer and plugged them in so they would have ample time to warm up.

While they warmed up, he went to work with his camera, placing it on the tripod and taking multiple pictures of himself against a plain white wall in his room. Once the equipment was warmed up, he carefully scanned both sides of the stolen license several times, looking for just the right copy. It took several tries, but it worked.

He then uploaded his photo and scanned license files onto his computer file. Next he resized the photo of himself and pasted it over the existing photo on the driver's license. He was completely impressed with his finished product. Once he printed both sides of the license he ran it through the laminator and was finished. When he was permanently settled, he would complete several of these licenses, finding the correct font, changing the name and superimposing other photos of himself in various differing disguises. The more he worked on this one, the more genius he felt. It was exhilarating.

For the time being, however, he needed only the one license and one blank passport. He enjoyed friendships, close friendships with several usable people in the State Department who 'owed' him. These unfortunate individuals were able to get him several blank passports along with the key to the chip in those passports. Getting their hands on not only the passport, but the key to the chip in the back of each one, matching the key to the passport, now that was impressive. His contacts never told him *how* they'd come into possession of these little beauties, he didn't care to know. It only mattered that he now had them. Bradford smiled as he pulled the first one out of the box. It felt good to have all the right connections. Whether or not it felt good to the man or woman on the other end of the agreement was none of his concern.

Once the license was complete, he took the passport and, using his printer, filled in the personal information via a program made to print like the State Department fonts and voila! He had a perfectly constructed passport to match his perfectly constructed driver's license. Maybe he would make a living doing this same thing for other people. This would be a good experiment to see how well they worked, though he had no doubt they would.

***

"Have you found the people responsible for your abduction yet?"

Neo, Sophia and Mrs. Barbosa sat together at the dining room table eating their dinner. After having them gone for so long, Neo always took a minute to enjoy the experience. He'd missed them, fought to get them back and would now appreciate them even more than he ever had.

"Not all of them. Those we've not arrested are most likely trying to get out of the country. Can't say a lot about it, of course, because it's an ongoing investigation, but just know, we're onto them and we'll get them. It's just a matter of time."

Sophia was quietly playing with her food.

"Is your stomach bothering you again tonight? Would you rather have some soup?" Neo worried about her eating enough food that would actually stay down. He couldn't believe pregnant women had the ability to feed a baby and themselves on the small amount of food they could keep inside them before it came up again.

"No, I'm fine, really," she said gazing at Neo with warm, moist eyes. "I was just thinking what you said in the warehouse when you rescued Mrs. Barbosa and me."

"What did I say?" Neo was trying to remember any words that came out of his mouth. He could only remember the anger.

"You said, 'He was standing just a little too close to my wife, and I didn't like it. So I shot him.' I was just thinking about how that made me feel."

"How did that make you feel?" Neo wasn't sure he wanted to hear the answer to that question.

"I felt...rescued. I felt like it didn't matter where I was or how dangerous a situation I was in, you would always come for me, and you would always rescue me." A single tear moved down her cheek as she smiled softly. "I felt, and still feel, very secure."

Neo reached out and took her hand. "I will always be there for you, Sophia. I will always come for you." Glancing across the table at a tearful cook, he said, "That goes for you, too, Mrs. Barbosa. You know that, right?"

With tears running down both cheeks, Mrs. Barbosa nodded her head in the positive, unable to actually speak...which was rare for the woman who had something to say about everything.

They finished their dinner and Mrs. Barbosa cleared the table and did the dishes. Tonight was a good night. Dinner stayed right where it was supposed to for Sophia. She didn't have even a little nausea.

Sophia and Neo moved from the table to the living room and settled in on the couch. The conversation quickly moved to names for the baby

"I like Nicole for a girl. What do you think?" Sophia stared expectantly at Neo

"Yes, Nicole is good, but it kind of sounds like nickel, don't you think?"

"Nickel?! Not at all. Nicole is a beautiful girl's name."

"Okay, then I get to name the boy, and I like the name Nathaniel."

Sophia smiled and laid her head on his shoulder. "I love that name. Maybe I'll hope for a boy."

Neo grabbed her and held her across his lap, staring into her large blue eyes. "Now, see how well that worked out?"

He pulled her up and kissed her soundly.

Chapter Eight

At a young twenty-nine years old, Aram Lincoln enjoyed his position as Legal Advisor to the Chief Operating Officer of the NSA, along with all the perks he could squeeze out of it. In a position to 'adjust' legal documents or 'position' events in such a way as to be what the rogue operatives needed them to be, he excelled at his job, both the legal and the illegal aspects. Because he worked closely with the Chief Financial Officer of the NSA, he was also able to skim funds where needed, though once the Markham family was out of the way, that was no longer a concern. Much had to be set up before that happened, however. The home in Mukilteo, Washington, had to be purchased prior to the abduction and that was quite expensive. The car the new persona, Neo Weston, would drive had to be purchased. It was an expensive op, and people were counting on Aram to get these important elements taken care of.

Born in Virginia, Aram was a U.S. citizen, however, his parents were Middle Eastern. His smooth brown skin accented his black hair and the coal black eyes indicative of his heritage. Very handsome with a chiseled jaw and always sporting a day's growth of beard, he became self-absorbed early on. He watched his parents work hard for every penny they earned. They never complained, but he knew in their hearts they were resentful. He never saw it, but how could they not be? *He* was certainly resentful. So many wealthy people, so many poor, and his parents were counted among the poor.

That was exactly why Aram decided to become a lawyer. Men in this profession often frequented his father's department store, buying a little here and a little there, capable of buying so much more had they wanted to. Were they just flaunting their wealth? He would one day flaunt his wealth as well.

He worked his way through college and then law school, never borrowing a penny. His parents were so proud, but *he* could never be proud of *them*. They bowed and scraped for every penny they earned, then what little they had extra they used toward Aram's schooling. It was embarrassing to him to see them so poor. He couldn't wait to leave the neighborhood and break out on his own, make a name for himself, *be* somebody.

Aram rolled onto his side in his large California king bed and gazed on the woman in bed next to him. Her name was…Hanna? Anna? Didn't matter. She had beautiful long dark lashes and soft brown hair that fell far below her shoulders. Her eyes were brown, but it wasn't just the color. The dark lashes around those eyes and the perfect almond shape were enough to steal any man's heart. Her face was a gentle oval, her smile lit up a room and everyone in it. However, he had a good hold on his heart. No woman would ever rule him. They were simply toys, and when this one was gone, there would be others. That was a given.

Yes, Aram had women in his life, all the women he wanted, anytime he wanted. They were practically standing in line to be with him. They were as pathetic as his parents. But they knew how important he was, knew how influential he was. They wanted to be with him because he was the right person to be with if they wanted to get anywhere in their lives. He'd offer them small visions into his life, show them a good time, then drop them when they became clingy or irritating, which didn't take long.

In his position as an attorney for the NSA, he hadn't seen the income he'd thought he'd see. He was frustrated in his job, working long hours to get ahead and getting nowhere. At least until Wesley Tipton and Tristan Bradford had come to him and invited him into the top-secret operation they were working. This operation would change his life, give him the means to have all the things in life he could want.

What Tipton and Bradford wanted was someone who could cover up a few things that might look out of place on a financial report, or remove evidence from the scene of a crime that could cause someone to look where they shouldn't. It wasn't anything very big, just small things, a little here and a little there. Soon he was covering the tracks of some of the NSA's top administrators, not to mention his own. The web he'd created became very hard to track, but it was necessary he keep up his work so none of them would be caught.

Then one day he received word Wesley Tipton was dead. No details, no clues, he was just dead. And not long after, Tristan Bradford disappeared. What was he supposed to do now? Would the op fall apart?

Was there another administrator waiting in the wings to take over this most lucrative operation? Maybe *he* should take it over. But how? He was only a small cog in a giant wheel. He didn't have all the facts, did he?

It was only when he started asking himself these hard questions that the horrifying thought came to him. What if someone had gone to the authorities with names and job titles? What if someone turned them all in?

That seemed ludicrous. He was above reproach. No one would ever know what he'd done anyway. He'd covered his activities far too well. Unless…unless someone kept a log of responsibilities he'd been assigned to 'take care of.' Why would they do that? It would get them into at *least* as much trouble as they'd get him into, probably more. A plea bargain. What if they made a plea bargain?

There was a knock at the door, and somewhere deep inside Aram's gut, he knew that wasn't a good thing. Sliding out of bed and into a robe, he walked out of the bedroom as he tied the sash. He opened the door slowly and, as suspected, there were four men standing in the hallway sporting dark suits and FBI badges, and all four of them had guns pointed right at him.

***

Cayman sighed and sat down at his desk. Neo came in moments later and sat down as well. The mood was definitely subdued, and even with the arrest of the rogue op's legal advisor, the two agents couldn't seem to be excited. Bradford had gone dark, no one had heard from him or seen him for weeks. His escape plan was ingenious…expensive, but ingenious. Somehow they had to find a lead on his whereabouts. The organization had pretty much crumbled and each day brought a new arrest. With two of the leadership dead, and two in custody, they were on their way to cleaning up the mess. There were five more out there, with leads leading to future arrests coming in every day. Still, it grated on a person, and both Cayman and Neo were feeling it.

"I've wanted to thank you for some time now, Cayman, for believing me. I know it must have sounded like some kind of sick joke when I called you that day in the coffee shop. I just didn't know who to turn to, and you didn't let me down." Neo's mouth turned up slightly at the corners, working very hard to lighten the feeling in the room.

"I have to admit, Neo, it was a leap of faith for me. But the minute I saw you and put that voice with you, I knew you were telling the truth. In fact, I've wanted to tell you for some time now, I feel like they made you *way* better looking, which must be a plus for Sophia."

"Nice. Just wait until someone grabs your millions, steals your life, and wipes not just your memory, but your face as well," said Neo, teasing his friend. "*Then* we'll see who's laughing." Neo chuckled softly, teasing. "In some ways, it was like getting a whole new start, you know. It can be so freeing."

Cayman smiled and folded his arms across his stomach as he leaned back in his chair. "You've had an amazing attitude about it, you know. You've never complained, not once. You've just set out to clean up the mess and you're doing the job very well. Because of your courage we're weeding out an operation that has poisoned the NSA for years now. They owe you a debt, and so does the FBI."

"Helping me keep my family safe is good enough payment for me."

There was a knock at Cayman's office door. "Come in."

"Aram Lincoln is in the interrogation room."

"Thanks, we'll be right there."

Cayman glanced at Neo. "Whose turn is it anyway?"

"I can't remember. Wanna flip for it? Kind of getting used to the same old song and dance. If they only knew how much we already know, maybe they'd skip the dance and just sing."

"I'll take the lead, you jump in any time."

They stood and headed into the hallway and down to the interrogation room.

A hopeful Aram Lincoln sat chained to the chair he sat in, anxious to be of assistance. He was already offering them aid before Neo and Cayman had a chance to sit down.

"I can give you anything you need, names, dates, places, anything. I have a great memory and I've taken some notes."

"I'm sure you have, Mr. Lincoln. But here's what we're thinking. We believe you're neck deep into a rogue operation involving, theft, kidnapping, murder and brainwashing. Now, if you have any information on any of *those* charges, we'd be happy to take it off your hands." Cayman crossed his arms over his chest and waited.

"I know nothing of any murder, kidnapping or brainwashing. Where are you getting your information?"

"What difference does it make where we got our information? We have it on good authority you're involved in this rogue op. We've confirmed your activities and we have proof of those activities. There's only one thing we need to know."

"What's that?"

"Where is Tristan Bradford?"

"If I knew that I certainly wouldn't be sitting here, now, would I? I'd have my hands around his scrawny neck watching him die."

"You've been very helpful. Have a nice prison life. You know how inmates *love* cops and attorneys. It's a beautiful thing."

Chapter Nine

Desmond Ashler was finally beginning to feel more human. It'd been a long recovery, after being beaten to near death, but saving Neo and Sophia was something he would feel proud of for the remainder of his days. He wasn't a top-notch agent nor was he administration in either the NSA or the FBI. He was simply a research physician, but finding out what happened to his best friend and getting him out of that situation was the best thing he'd ever done, and he'd do it again without thinking twice.

He was finally able to get around on his own, and he needed only small amounts of help every now and then with standing from a sitting position or balancing. Ciara had been an incredible help in his recovery. He watched her walking toward him and felt such comfort in having her close.

Ciara approached the easy chair with confidence. Desmond knew how much easier it was for her now that he was able to walk without the walker. She leaned over, as she usually did, kissed him on the forehead and stood up, placing her hands under his arms and clasping them gently behind his back to steady him as he worked to get out of the chair. He placed his feet firmly on the floor and stood slowly, taking his time and making sure he was steady before starting out.

Unfortunately, *this* was one of those occasions where Desmond's balance was just a little off. Desmond's eyes widened as he felt himself falling backward onto the chair. Out of sheer self-preservation, he put both arms around Ciara, and she fell forward onto him as he fell into the chair. Immediately the footrest jumped from the bottom of the chair into the full open position as the chair fell backward onto the floor.

So there they were, Desmond laid out on the chair which was laid out on the floor, and Ciara laid out on Desmond, their feet straight up in the air. He gazed up into her most surprised face and began to laugh. He couldn't help it. When he could speak he said, "Well, that's wasn't as much fun as I thought it would be. Except that it *is* pretty cozy, don't you think?"

Ciara slapped his shoulder and barked, "Stop laughing and help me get me off of this thing!" Desmond, unable to move anything, was beginning to shriek with uproarious giggles and Ciara couldn't help joining in. "I mean it Desmond. I'm...I'm...stuck and I can't...move." She was saying each word as best she could between peals of laughter, worried at the same time she might hurt him if she moved wrong.

Pushing off from the armrests, Ciara struggled to move her body to the side of Desmond and his upside-down chair. As she was doing so, Desmond took her by the waist and lifted just slightly. However, his arms were still quite weak causing Ciara to slip from his grasp. As she did, she slid, not so gracefully, onto the floor beside the chair with an 'ooomf'. When she stood, she burst into wild howls as she stared at her gorgeous fiancé, head on the chair back, which was still on the floor with his feet on the footrest, which remained straight up in the air. She went limp, and collapsed on the floor trying to quell the peals of hilarity that burst from her gut.

"Okay, it was funny, but now I can't get up and you're going to have to right this chair."

Still laughing, she nodded and forced herself to her feet. She moved slowly, half crawling, half walking to the head of the chair. Unaware of her own strength, she stood and took a deep breath. She grabbed the chair back and lifted with all her might. As luck would have it, the easy chair wasn't as heavy as she'd thought it would be. In fact, it was quite light. The chair back flew up from the floor and past the upright position, depositing Desmond on the floor in front of it. The footrest snapped into place before the chair landed upside down on Desmond's back, pinning him to the floor.

"Oh! Honey! I'm so sorry! I didn't know it would do that, I was-" She came around the side of the chair to see Desmond flat on the ground, trying to reach behind him with one arm to get the chair off and she nearly collapsed on the floor beside him once again. Lifting and pulling the chair back to its upright position, she fell to the floor by Desmond, trying as hard as she could to be compassionate and not laugh.

"Baby, are you okay?"

"It's a good thing this doesn't hurt," he said, as he pushed himself up and rolled onto his side. Locking his elbow, he held himself in place with a straight arm propped on the floor and stared at the now righted easy chair. "There were parts of that situation that were really quite satisfying."

"You are totally hopeless, you know that? I'm just glad we didn't re-break anything."

The two of them worked at bringing Desmond back to a standing position, this time from the floor and not from the chair. It was hard work and with a lot of grunting and sweating he finally stood before her.

"If anyone were standing on the other side of that door," he said, breathless and pointing to their front door, "they would *not* think we were upright."

Ciara giggled and shook her head. "Are you ready to try walking to the table or are you going to stand here and daydream all day?"

"The daydreaming was kind of nice. Maybe I'll stay right here."

"Uh, huh."

***

Leon Kenning remembered the feeling of coming out of the fog of his PTSD. Badly beaten, but not as severely as his friend and associate Desmond, Leon knew himself to be suffering from PTSD. He knew what the symptoms were and what needed to be done, but being the patient instead of the doctor had opened his eyes to a whole new view of the disorder. Somehow, he couldn't bring Leon, the patient, to do anything he knew needed to be done. He felt…emotionally paralyzed, unable to think clearly, to formulate even the most basic plan for healing. He was thankful to his therapist, Rachel, for standing by him and keeping him focused on his recovery and *not* on his psychiatrist. Hard though that was, he was thankful for her wisdom and professionalism.

On this night, however, Leon sat at his desk, barely aware of his surroundings. His palms were sweating, his heart pounding, knowing the door to his office would open at any moment.

After dinner with Rachel the evening before, and with a very light heart, Leon decided he would buy a wedding ring set the following day, which he'd done, with plans to present it to her at dinner that night. *What was I thinking?*

What if he'd totally read her wrong? What if the signals she was sending meant 'you're fun, but I like being single?' He adjusted his shoulders, breathing deeply and trying to calm his escalating blood pressure. It didn't help. *People actually went through this every day? Are they crazy?* Attempting to force himself to think rationally, he realized people hopefully only have to do this once in a lifetime. They'd have to be stupid to do it more than once.

Grabbing a tissue from the box on his desk, he dabbed his face and forehead. He glanced up at the clock. She was late. It was 5:02 and she was supposed to be here promptly at 5:00. Could he live with this kind of tardiness? That was something he'd really have to think on. He decided he'd need to wait at least another twenty-four hours and see how this played out. Then there was her sense of fashion. Clothes like that don't come cheap. Maybe he couldn't *afford* to marry this woman. Maybe she'd drive him straight into bankruptcy.

And what about that perfume she wore? He didn't even *want* to know what that cost. Anything that intoxicating had to be exp -

The door opened and Rachel's smile entered the room. The smile was wearing a perfectly fitted red dress that followed every smooth, flowing curve of her body. As she approached the desk, he could smell the incredible scent that embodied all that made her who she was. He watched her sway slowly toward him, wondering if maybe it wasn't the other way around. Maybe all that she was made the scent so very intoxicating, the dress so...red.

He stood as she reached his desk and she sank into his arms like hot fudge over ice cream. He was the ice cream, and the essence of her melted over him, filling his senses with her scent, her softness, her warmth. Their lips met and every frightening thought was gone. She was all that was left.

He now knew he would never be complete without her. She was his North Star, the focal point on his life's compass. It was as if he'd been guided through life for the sole purpose of finding her, and she him. Without thought or coaxing, the words poured from his mouth.

"Marry me, Rachel."

She gazed softly into his eyes, as if seeing them for the first time. The intensity in that gaze filled him with longing, with desire. He was no longer afraid of her answer.

Seconds passed and she pressed her lips to his, once again. Fierce passion pulsated through them, forging a burning inside him that could not be extinguished. She finally released his mouth and smiled that incredibly sexy, motivating smile.

"I thought you'd never ask."

Chapter Ten

Abe Spencer, Deputy Chief Operating Officer for Military Affairs for the NSA, was sixty-two years old on his last birthday. He was a big man, a good eighty pounds overweight and out of condition. Fast approaching retirement, he'd worked a lifetime, never able to make the money he'd once dreamed of, always ending up two feet away from the goal. When he didn't come through with the 'good life' for his wife, she left him for a rich man twice her age and took their two children with her. Now the children refused to speak to their dad, considering him lazy and uninspired.

The grandson of immigrants, Abe watched his grandparents and his father work hard to make a life in America when he was very young. His father spoke of the Great Depression like it was some kind of magical, dream-sucking cloud that covered the earth. It had stolen their sole source of income and left them destitute. As a child, Abe didn't realize how many were affected by it and felt this 'depression' was an evil meant only for his family.

Abe grew up bitter and angry at the loss of what was supposed to be his family's fortune. He became greedy, hanging on to every bit of money that came his way, only to have to draw it out of his savings to pay for doctor bills for kids or a new car or a down payment on a home. He could never get ahead, no matter how hard he tried. And he tried plenty hard.

His ex-wife, now she was a different story. As soon as he made the money, she spent it. Clothes, jewelry, accessories, you name it. If it cost money, she had to have it, and the more it cost the more she wanted it. She'd bled him dry from the day they married. Now any extra he had went to pay off years of divorce lawyers and mediation specialists. They were divorced now five years and she was *still* bleeding him dry.

When Bradford approached Abe, Abe knew right away what Bradford was asking was incredibly illegal, and he didn't care. He'd already lost everything that ever mattered to him, so what else was there to lose? Maybe he could buy his children's love back from their money grubbing mother.

Abe stashed the money he earned in a large safe at his house, lest he be investigated for some meaningless infringement and his bank account not match his income level. He'd amassed a small fortune and was quite proud of his accomplishment. His retirement plans involved a home, a mansion really, in the great country of Chile. He'd paid cash for the property as an 'undisclosed buyer' in an effort to keep the purchase under wraps. Aram Lincoln helped him with the purchase.

Having been down to Chile on several occasions, Abe enjoyed throwing his money around and talking like a big man. He'd had women, expensive wine and the respect and groveling of the poor in the city. He felt like he was *somebody* down there. His generosity was well known, but every beggar knew to stay off his property. Those who crossed the property line to knock at the door for food or handouts never returned. Yes, he was generous, but he was also feared. That fear made him feel even more powerful, and that power made him anxious to get back down there for a permanent stay.

The leadership of the rogue operation was disappearing. Some were dead and some arrested. Others were just gone. He was going to be one of the 'just gone' leaders, and that meant leaving today. He couldn't risk discovery and losing everything he'd worked so hard for.

Lines of sweat ran down his face as he hurriedly packed what little he thought he'd need. He grabbed his passport and fake ID, leaving his current driver's license and ID on his bed. They could find it if they wanted to look. He didn't care. He'd deposited his cash in small increments over the last two months into overseas accounts and everything was in place for his exodus. He was out of here.

With only one small carry-on bag, he rushed to his car, heading to Dulles for the next flight to Chile. He was excited beyond belief, but anxiety also filled him. Had they found him out yet? Were they on their way to arrest him, like the others? He needed to disappear and should have done this weeks ago. It was just so hard to believe it was over. Now he could believe it. It was over.

Fighting the urge to spin out at every stoplight and take off, he maintained a legal speed and turned on the radio to help him be calm. Checking the rearview mirror, he saw a dark SUV following him. Was he being paranoid? Were they there for him? *Don't be a fool. Stay calm and just keep going.*

He turned down a street to see if the SUV followed him and it did. A couple of turns later, Abe was convinced he was being followed, and he knew what that meant. In a panic, he drove to a low-income subdivision, and weaving through the streets, he lost the tail for a short while, long enough for him to park and run through several backyards before finding a home he thought was vacant. He would lie low there for a few hours and then call a taxi to get him to the airport. No matter if he had to change his flight. He was under no time constraints to get there; a flight change would be of no consequence.

Abe broke open the door with a kick and rushed into the house to find a terrified woman in the kitchen. She screamed at the noise and began to run out of the kitchen. Abe grabbed her and held her fast, placing his large hand over her mouth.

"Stay quiet and I let you live, scream and you die. Are we clear?"

The woman nodded her head, her long brown hair covering part of her face. Abe slowly released her mouth and she whispered, "I have a baby. He's napping. Please don't hurt him."

"I'm not here to hurt you or your baby. I just need a place to hide for a couple hours. Go shut your living room curtains."

"I…I don't have any curtains. We just moved in a week ago and we haven't gotten any yet."

"Then go get a sheet, or a blanket, anything. Cover the window. Now." Abe's voice was low and threatening. He could see he was scaring her, but he didn't care. He had a plan, and no one was going to interfere with it.

The woman rushed away, and returned with two large flat sheets, placing them over the window as fast as she could. Abe stayed hidden while she worked, unaware of the two men approaching the house. They motioned to the woman, asking her with hand signs if there was a man in there. She nodded in the affirmative and they motioned again, mouthing for her to stay calm.

"What's taking so long in there? Hurry up."

The woman jumped and said, "It's hard for me to reach, I'm almost done." She reached up and tucked the final corner of the second sheet over the existing curtain rod and secured it in place. "Okay, it's finished."

Her demeanor was changed. She wasn't as frightened and she seemed angry. What made her change so suddenly? Abe was instantly suspicious.

***

Cayman and Neo had just finished a quick lunch when the call came in from dispatch that there was a pursuit in progress. The suspect was Abe Spencer and agents were able to determine the suspect was holed up in a home not far from the airport. There was at least one hostage.

The two rushed to the scene and found several SUV's parked in front of a small home. They exited the car and found Spencer holding a gun to the head of a woman in front of a large picture glass window inside the home. He stood to the left side of the window, with only the gun showing. On either side of the large window were two smaller windows that could be opened. The left one was open and an infant's cry could be heard.

"I'm going around the back," said Neo.

"Take some men with you," said Cayman softly, nodding toward several agents standing behind cars for protection.

"I think it's better if I go alone. Keep him busy on this side."

"Neo, you need - "

"Cayman, I work better alone. I don't want to be responsible for anyone else getting hurt. Let me do this."

"Go, we'll watch the front." Cayman didn't have time to argue with him and knew Neo was right anyway.

Neo moved slowly to the left side of the home. When he was out of the shooter's line of sight, he moved quickly to the back, taking up a position beside another large window that looked out onto the backyard. He peeked slowly around the window frame and saw the suspect holding the gun. He could hear the child's frantic cries for his mother, and a switch flipped inside of him. He had to protect the child and its mother.

Crawling under the window to the garage door, he quietly opened the door and crept inside. He could hear the suspect telling the agents to leave or he would kill the woman. He tried making demands, a helicopter to take him to the airport, a SUV to drive to Dulles…the demands were random and were more like someone thinking out loud.

Neo slowly turned the handle on the kitchen door and entered. He was close enough now he could hear the man breathing. He lifted his handgun to eye level and began walking forward, slowly. When he appeared in the kitchen, Spencer grabbed the woman and pulled her in front of him, shielding him from Neo.

The woman screamed and tried to fight, but Spencer was too big. Neo watched her plant her feet like someone who'd had some training in self-defense.

"Abe, do you know who I am?"

"No, and if you don't get out of here, this little lady is going to die."

"My name was Justin Markham, until your little group got a hold of me. If you know anything about Justin Markham, you know I'm a highly-trained, incredibly accurate sniper, and you have to realize this is going to end very badly for you."

"You're not Justin Markham. I know what he looks like, and he's not you."

"That's right, Abe. The men who took me changed my facial features. The only thing they couldn't change is my height, and the fact that I still know how to kill a man from over seven hundred feet. Imagine what I can do from fifteen. I can take your head right off your neck, and you know that's true."

Spencer's gun wavered between the woman and Neo, as if he was unsure who he should aim at. If Spencer became too agitated, the gun would fire and the hostage was the one who would take that hit, Neo was sure of it.

Neo saw the woman focused on his face. She was waiting for a cue from him so she could get out of the way. Timing the movement of Spencer's hand, he nodded to her when the gun was pointing away from her, barely moving his head. In a movement smooth and calculated, the woman stomped on the foot of her attacker with all her might, then dropped immediately to the floor, rolling quickly away from him.

A shot rang out from Spencer's gun, but Neo fired first and the man fell to the floor. The woman jumped up and ran into the hallway, to her child's room. She came out of the room holding the tiny bundle, calming him and bouncing him softly.

"I'm sorry you had to go through this. Would you like to have the baby looked at? I can make arrangements for that."

"No, he's fine. Thank you, though."

The agents barreled through the door one by one with guns raised.

"It's over," said Neo as they entered. "You're going to need a body bag."

Chapter Eleven

Drew Baldwin, Global Network Advisor to the Signals Intelligence Mission Director for the NSA, began his day much the same way as he did any other day. With sandy blonde hair and green eyes, Drew looked like a twelve year old instead of the twenty-eight year old he was. Being shorter than most everyone around him did nothing to make him appear his age.

On this day, he kissed his wife, Emma Jean, and two-year old daughter, Shayla, goodbye and left for work. He considered himself a blessed man, with a loving family and a nice home in a great neighborhood. His neighbors watched out for each other, which was very nice.

Emma Jean and Shayla were his world. He worked only to support them, but his real joy came from having them in his life. His evenings at home were spent on the floor of their living room, playing with his baby girl. He loved to hear her laugh, to make her laugh and to make her absolutely aware of her father's love for her. In his whole life, he swore to himself that he would never, ever be too busy for his wife or his children. He was devoted to making their world safe and filled with love, and he worked very hard at it.

That was exactly why, when an associate, Aram Lincoln, came to him asking for his help with a highly classified op, one that would make the country safer for families such as his, he jumped at the opportunity to help. Aram paid him directly, with cash, saying the op was so confidential it was necessary to pay him with cash. Aram was the attorney for the NSA and Drew trusted him implicitly. If there was anything about the op that was illegal, Drew could count on Aram to make him aware of it.

When he was paid the first time, it was an amazing amount of money, and Drew thought maybe he should tell his superiors, but then he wondered if he was being tested in his ability to follow orders. He wasn't really trained as an agent, and was unsure what constituted disobeying orders on an 'op.' He decided he would definitely trust his co-worker and maintain the confidentiality, showing those at the top what he was capable of.

When he'd told Emma Jean of their good fortune, she was excited at the prospects the extra money would bring to their family. Immediately they began to put the money away for a down payment on their home and a college fund for Shayla. Their new home, the one they currently lived in, had three more bedrooms, which would allow their family to grow without them having to move again. That was the best part of buying a new home. They wanted their children to grow up in the same home and bring their families back to the house they grew up in. Both Drew and Emma Jean wanted that sense of family and feeling of stability for their children.

However, it didn't take long for Drew to begin to question some of the things he was being asked to do. He approached Aram with his concerns, but was assured everything was as it should be. Aram explained to him the need to keep this op out of the eye of anyone who wasn't a part of it. The ramifications of their actions were too hard for anyone not on the team to understand, and it couldn't be explained to them without divulging classified information. Drew was made aware only of his part in the operation. He had but one small part to do and, as Aram had explained, it was a very important part.

Drew's responsibility was to make sure any reference to the work the team did was kept off the network. It required constant scanning of the system, setting up programs with code words that could be tracked so the team would know if anyone was aware of their work. If Drew found any references to the operation, he was to forward it on to Aram and then delete it off the network. It definitely wasn't hard, but it just seemed...wrong. His best explanation for it was that most likely all of these highly classified operations felt wrong. It gave him little comfort, but it helped.

One day he was particularly bothered when he overheard people talking in the hallway about Aram and how he'd been arrested by the FBI for kidnapping and murder. Drew was shocked, his legs instantly going weak. He leaned against the wall for support, staring at some papers he was carrying, listening to the conversations. The more he heard, the sicker his stomach felt. Murder? Kidnapping? What? How-? When-? He didn't even know what questions to ask. Was this the same op Drew was involved in himself?

If it was, he had to turn himself in right away. He had to let the FBI know he was part of it, but the shame he felt was almost unbearable. Had he really been a party to murder and kidnapping?

Trying to gain the strength to do what he felt he had to do, Drew took a deep breath and hurried back to his office. The first thing he did was sit down at his desk and call Emma Jean. He explained he'd not be home for dinner and to be sure and kiss Shayla goodnight for him. He told her he'd call as soon as he could.

"What's happened, Drew? Why are you being so secretive?"

"Please, Emma Jean, I will explain it all as soon as I understand it myself. Do you trust me?"

"Yes, of course I trust you."

"Then just know that I will call you as soon as I can. And know one more thing. Always know that I love you and Shayla."

Drew ended the call, picked up his coat, his briefcase and walked with leaded feet to his car. He got in, started the car and drove directly to the Hoover building. He wasn't exactly sure what he'd done, but he figured he'd find out soon enough.

***

Neo felt bad for this suspect. The poor man was so distraught Neo couldn't bring himself to take him to an interrogation room, instead directing him into the conference room. It looked as if Drew Baldwin had been taken for a serious ride. If that weren't the case, why was he here? Did he understand what he was copping to? Neo had his doubts. Although, it was an interesting turn of events to have one of the rogue team of agents walk into the Bureau and pretty much say, "'cuff me, I'm guilty," which was the main reason Neo wanted to hear this guy's story.

This was a good man, a family man and he'd been used in the worst way. He'd been taken advantage of by his peers for the knowledge he had and paid a tiny portion of what others were being paid, accepting just as much risk. Clearly he had no idea what the organization was doing and how far they'd gone. The poor man was shaking so hard when he displayed his badge to Neo that it could hardly be read.

"Maybe you could start by telling me what you do at the NSA, Mr. Baldwin." Neo waited, fairly sure the man would pass out before he could answer. But he didn't pass out.

"I…uh…I'm the… I work with the…well, I'm not…I don't really…."

Neo interrupted. "What is your job title, Mr. Baldwin?"

"Yes, yes, well, I'm the Global Network Advisor to the Signals Intelligence Mission Director." He took a deep breath, looking pleased he'd actually been able to get something intelligent out of his mouth.

"And in that position, what are your job responsibilities?"

"I, uh, I'm over the, uh, the networks." He slowly became more confident and began to speak more coherently. "I monitor the networks, schedule maintenance and oversee that maintenance. If a special network set up is needed I either do that myself or oversee the set up by my people. I thought that's why these people contacted me, why they wanted me to set up a network specifically for their op. That's not an unreal request for my position."

Neo studied Drew for a moment before speaking. "Who was your contact for the op?"

"I...I didn't really have a contact...I mean, not like a person on those spy movies or anything. Aram Lincoln asked me if I would assist him and offered me money. He swore me to secrecy, though, telling me he'd pay me cash because the op was highly classified and there could be no trail left to anyone in the op. He said it was for our own protection. Aram was our Legal Advisor and I trusted him."

With that, Drew's eyes focused on Neo's face, as lights went on inside his head. "I trusted him," he whispered. "Was he lying to me the whole time?"

Neo could see he was losing Drew and needed to keep him present in the interview. "Mr. Baldwin, it might help to concentrate on one thing at a time. Can you do that for me?"

Drew's eyes snapped back to the present and he cleared his throat. "Yes, yes, you're right. It's just that I have a family, my wife and our little girl. They depend on me for support. I...I didn't know I was doing anything wrong. I really didn't."

"Listen, Mr. Baldwin, let me just say, I think you're okay. I don't think you're responsible for what this rogue operation was and what they did. I can see you were sucked in with the use of lies and manipulation. Now, having said that, I need to know what Aram Lincoln asked you to do for him."

Drew took a deep breath and began. "When Aram approached me, he asked if it was possible for me to set up a separate network for an ultra-classified operation that was going to need invisibility, even to the NSA. I thought this was pretty weird, because how can the administration monitor an operation they can't see? The way it was explained to me was that they had authorization from these leaders, right up to Tristan Bradford, to do whatever it took to make this operation a success. I was never told what the whole operation entailed. It was my understanding that each cog in the wheel wasn't aware of what the other cogs did."

Neo nodded his head. "I see. Did anyone else ever approach you about this 'op?' Did anyone ever ask you about it or question you about it?"

Drew's eyes grew wide. "No, not ever and if they had, I was told by Aram that I was to deny any knowledge of it."

An agent entered the conference room and whispered into Neo's ear. Neo nodded in the affirmative as the man spoke and when he left, Neo stood.

"I'm sorry Mr. Baldwin, but we're going to have to cut this interview short. You are free to go, but please don't leave the state. We will probably need to speak with you again."

"I'm…I'm free to go? But this group did very bad things!"

"Yes, they did, Mr. Baldwin, but you had no knowledge of that. I can see you're telling the truth. Just stay close and be available if we should call you."

"I will, I definitely will," said Drew, standing and shaking Neo's hand. Neo directed him out the door and then headed to Cayman's office.

"What's going on? Bingham said we had a multiple suicide?"

"Yes, as it happens, it's the three names on the list we hadn't gotten to yet. I guess as they saw the structure of their organization tumble, they couldn't deal with the consequences *they* would have, so they took matters into their own hands. Are you up for a look?"

"Yup. Let's go see the bad news."

Chapter Twelve

Neo drove this time and they headed out of the parking garage for a home in a Bethesda subdivision. As they arrived they saw the coroner's van and several police cars, along with two FBI SUVs.

As they exited their car a local policeman approached. "Are you with the FBI?"

Both men showed him their badge. "Yes, we are. What's happened here?"

The policeman began. "First look this appears to be a suicide. Three men got into the car, left the garage door shut, turned on the engine and that was that. However, the coroner may have different information for you. She's just over here, let me introduce you."

The coroner was a female, petite with dark hair and dark eyes. She was suited up for examination of the bodies, wearing the familiar white jumpsuit.

The officer did the introductions. "Dr. Arianna Lewis, these are Agents Richards and Weston from the Bureau."

"Nice to meet you. Let me show you what I've found." She led them to the garage where the car was parked and to the driver's side door, which was open. "Mind you, I can't be sure of any of this until I have them on my table, but to me, it looks like some petechial hemorrhaging in the eyes and face. I'd be willing to bet they were asphyxiated prior to being placed in the car. The hemorrhaging is subtle, and like I said, I'll be able to tell more when I get them to the lab."

She looked up at the men and cocked her head to one side. "Do either one of you know a Justin Markham?"

"Yes," replied Neo. "I know him."

She looked at him, recognizing the second of hesitation on his part before answering. "Well, whoever did this knows him. There's a note in the pocket of the driver. I can only see the name, so the note may not be *for* him, but *about* him. I didn't want to disturb the scene until I had the go ahead from you guys." She handed Neo a pair of exam gloves as she spoke.

Neo struggled into the gloves. Once they were on, he reached into the car and pulled the note from the pocket of the deceased. The note had been written in a hurry.

"Justin Markham: You have something I want, and I intend to get it from you."

Neo nodded to Cayman and Cayman turned to Dr. Lewis. "We'll stop by later and review your findings if that works for you."

"I'll be ready. Thanks."

The two men didn't speak until they were in the car, then it was Cayman who began.

"What was in the note?"

Neo held the note in his gloved hands for Cayman to see. Cayman read it and leaned back in the seat, resting his head on his hand, his elbow propped against his door. Neo was beyond words.

"What am I going to tell Sophia? She's going to be terrified."

"Is there any chance you wouldn't tell her? Might be easier on her if she doesn't know."

Neo sighed. "We made a promise to each other when we married…no more secrets. By keeping her a secret from my work, it almost cost us a relationship. I don't know if I could or should keep this from her. She has a right to know, because she may be in as much danger as I am. Hiding her does little to no good. Moving her again? That would just be out of the question. Now with the baby coming, I'm not sure, maybe she would rather move again and stay in hiding. Bottom line is we have to find Bradford before Bradford finds me. I don't know what else to do, do you?"

Cayman ran his hands through his hair. "You must be so tired of this."

"You could say that, yes."

This had been the longest, the most tedious op Neo had ever been a part of. Once these three men were identified, the operation would be all but closed, except for one not-so-small detail. Tristan Bradford. How he hated that name, and the man who hid behind it. Once powerful and in control, Bradford had withered to threats and murder and more threats, jumping from the shadows to strike and running back into hiding like the money-grubbing coward he really was. How do you fight someone who's invisible?

Neo came out of his thoughts with a question. "What is the status of your snitches? You have any that might have heard something about Bradford? Anything?"

"That's an excellent idea. I may have someone. Let me see if I can locate him and we'll go pay him a visit."

They drove back to the Hoover building and Cayman headed to his office. Neo followed him.

"Cayman, I'm going to head home for a bit, see if I can talk to Sophia. I'm going to have to talk to Mrs. Barbosa, as well, they both have a right to know."

"Sounds good, I'll wait for you here."

Neo drove the short distance to the penthouse and rode the elevator up, deep in thought, wondering how he was going to tell them they were, once again, on the run. It just didn't seem right. *Every time we think we're about free of this cursed discovery of mine, we find out we're not.* It was beginning to feel like the same old song and dance, except for the very real threats that came along with it.

When the elevator doors opened, Sam and Patrick lay unconscious on the floor, the all too familiar tranquilizer darts sticking from their necks. Neo's heart skipped a beat as he started for the door. He checked the pulse of both men, noting a steady, but slowed, beat. The door into the penthouse was opened just a crack and Neo peeked inside and saw his wife curled up comfortably on the sofa reading a book. He heard Mrs. Barbosa humming contentedly from the kitchen. *Are they aware the door is open?*

Neo dialed Cayman's phone.

"Richards."

Speaking softly he said into the phone, "Get to my penthouse ASAP, two agents down, bring backup."

The line went dead without another word.

Neo's heart was pounding, his emotions raging from fear for his family to outrage at the sheer audacity of Bradford. He knew this was Bradford's work, it had to be.

Peeking his head through the door, he noticed a sealed envelope on the floor at his feet. He bent over and picked it up, recognizing the handwriting immediately. He stuffed the note in his pocket.

"Hey, handsome," Sophia stood and stretched. "What are you doing home so early?"

Neo held his finger to his lips, motioning for her to say nothing. He drew his gun and stepped inside the door, leaving it open. Sophia saw Patrick and Sam lying on the floor and she gasped, her eyes widening. He motioned for Sophia to go into the kitchen with Mrs. Barbosa, which she did very quickly. He then motioned for the two women to get down on the floor behind the island.

Neo made his way silently through the house, checking all the rooms and closets. He'd found nothing until he stepped into the master bathroom and looked at the mirror.

***

Four FBI vehicles pulled up in front of the building that housed Neo and Sophia's penthouse, along with an ambulance, sirens blaring. Cayman raced into the building. He motioned to his team to spread out and search the floor. He sent another team to check the stairwells and kept four men with him.

They entered the elevator, checking it carefully first, and rode it to the top floor.

When the door opened, both Patrick and Sam were coming around. Neo was with them and was helping them sit up against the wall.

"How long have you been here?" Cayman was watching his brothers coming to as he spoke to Neo.

"I'm not sure, probably five minutes, maybe eight."

"He must have had a pretty light dose of tranquilizer in those guns."

"I have no idea how long ago he was in the house, but I'm so glad Sophia didn't see the bathroom mirror without me here. I better go talk to her."

Neo and Cayman left Patrick and Sam in the capable hands of the EMTs who'd just arrived. They entered the penthouse, shutting the door behind them.

Sophia was doing her best to maintain some sense of calm, but she was losing it quickly. She rushed to Neo, throwing her arms around his neck and the sobbing began.

"No, Neo. No."

"I'm sorry, Sophia. I'm so sorry."

Mrs. Barbosa came around the counter and stood solemnly, saying nothing. Neo motioned for her to join them and she came to the two of them, wrapping her arms around them.

Cayman stepped back to give them some privacy. He walked to the huge windows overlooking D.C. and gazed out. How does one fight a ghost?

***

Neo had no words as the three of them embraced. They'd been through this so many times; it was ridiculous to think of hiding again. But Bradford had proven his point. He could've hurt Neo's family, but he didn't. Why? Just to prove that he could if he wanted to? It would seem that was the case, and at this point, Neo didn't care what his reasoning was. He was only thankful his family was safe.

Neo released the women. "Cayman, follow me. Sophia, you and Mrs. Barbosa wait here." He motioned for two agents to come into the house from the hallway. "Stay with them, please." The men nodded.

He directed Cayman into the master bathroom and showed him the mirror. Letters scrawled in bright red lipstick glared out from the mirror. They read the message silently. *"I WON'T WAIT LONG."*

The words reminded Neo of the note he'd stuffed in his pocket.

"Oh, and I found this on the floor inside the door to the penthouse." He opened the note and pulled out the paper by a tiny corner, laying the note on the bathroom counter. He gingerly unfolded the sheet of paper and read the note.

"See how easy this was, Justin? You have something I want. I intend to get it from you. Don't make me do something we'll both regret. Send the executable file for the algorithm to 'XP7LT@maildrop.cc' and we'll call it good."

Cayman could see the intensity on Neo's face. The muscles in his jaw twitched as he stared at the paper, his eyes could've burned holes right through it. Cayman weighed his words carefully.

"The next step has to be your call, Neo. We can send you all into witness protection again, or just the women, or no one. It's up to you."

Neo turned his back to the note and leaned against the counter, arms folded across his chest.

"That front door is the only entrance into the penthouse." Neo was thinking out loud as he stared at the floor.

"Are you asking me or telling me?"

"I guess I'm telling *me*," he said, raising his head. His eyes had a distant look. "I feel like we need to keep my family where they are, and up the security. We could do the same thing we did with Desmond and Ciara."

Neo's glare hardened as he turned to Cayman. "We need to check with the team at their place, and check with Leon, as well…we need to make sure they're all okay."

"I'll make the calls and be right back." Cayman left the room and Neo stood alone in the quiet.

He turned back to the note, placing his hands against the side of the countertop and leaning against it with arms locked. He didn't look at the note; he lowered his head and stared at the floor.

Bradford was really beginning to get under his skin. Logically, the sniper in him told him that was a bad thing. He shouldn't let this man get to him. Until now he'd never had an issue with that. Now he did. Now he had a family, and Sophia was actually not just Sophia anymore. She was carrying their child now. Mrs. Barbosa was older, and he worried about keeping her living on the edge like this. Her nerves were frazzled, but he already knew the response he'd get from her if he tried to separate her from the family.

She was as much a part of the family as the baby Sophia carried inside her.

How was he supposed to fight this? How was he supposed to protect his family from someone like Bradford? One clear shot. All it would take was one clear shot and it would all be over. But Neo knew he couldn't start thinking like that. There was a fine line between a sniper and a killer, and that was the line. 'One clear shot.' He understood what the implications were of that phrase. He was taking away the man's right to a trial. He was making himself judge, jury and executioner. Oh, how good that sounded to him right at this moment. But life went on after this moment, and so would his family. *And so would his family.*

Chapter Thirteen

Cayman instructed his team to go by the homes of Leon and Desmond. He wanted them to do a physical check of the residences. "If Leon isn't home, and I suspect he's at work, then go to his office after checking his home. On your way to the residences, call the team at the hotel. Make sure it's quiet."

Cayman and Neo sat in his office once again. Leon, Desmond and Ciara were fine; the guards at the hotel were still in place. It appeared Bradford had one goal in mind. He wanted what was in Neo's head. It occurred to Neo after reading and re-reading the notes that Bradford was after only one thing. He considered everything between him and the algorithm inconsequential, disposable.

Neo knew how Bradford thought, and that knowledge sent a chill through him. This line of thinking made the assailant a very dangerous man. As the walls closed in around him, a dangerous man could become a desperate man, and that was something Neo wanted to avoid, if it could be avoided.

Now even deeper into his own head, Neo knew Bradford couldn't be trusted. If Neo *did* email him the algorithm, how could he know the deal would be done? What if he couldn't get it to work? He wasn't a computer man, which meant he was going to need someone to run the code and see if it worked. Did he have people he could call on for that kind of help? Was there anything left of his network? Neo realized with a sigh this ordeal was far from over. Even if he emailed the algorithm it didn't guarantee his family's safety.

Neo sat forward, his whole body snapping to attention. A mischievous smile spread slowly across his face and he stared at his friend. "Cayman, I think I have an idea."

Cayman looked at him with more than surprise. "Neo, what are you thinking? What's with the big smile?"

"How's Emmett feeling these days?" Neo glanced at Cayman, still smiling.

"He's feeling a little cooped up, still in lockup and being treated like a traitor."

"I think he needs to escape our custody. His escape will be very ingenious and once he's out he's going to make contact with Bradford. We'll give him a real bad boy prison persona and make sure he has *all kinds* of bogus information to feed his new 'boss.' Whadaya think?"

Cayman smiled widely. "I like it. I really like it."

The last time Neo felt this relieved, this relaxed, he was lying on a beach outside his mansion at sunset with his wife beside him. He could almost feel that setting sun on his skin at this moment.

***

The guard made his rounds of the cellblock each day, checking on prisoners and making sure everyone was where they should be. Emmett watched him, waiting for his moment. How would this all play out? He'd been told he'd know the moment when it came and to be vigilant.

Today he lay on his bunk, watching carefully as the guard strolled by. Nothing happened.

Suddenly the loud buzz that announced the opening of the cell doors sounded in his ears. He knew the routine. Prisoners were to walk to their door and stand with hands at their side as the doors slid open. When instructed, they could exit their cells and walk single-file from the block. Usually this signaled time in the yard, but it wasn't the right time of day for that. He could hear the other prisoners murmuring. Emmett was alert; watching and listening for any clue that would tell him his prison break was imminent. He stood quickly and walked to the door.

This escape would be no picnic for him. In fact, it would be very dangerous. He'd been briefed on how it would go down, but the path that would be cleared for him wasn't a sure thing. He'd have to play it by ear. As was usually the case, once he'd cleared the prison, every state and city agency would be on the lookout for him. They would be ordered to bring him in alive, but that was just the order. Escaping felons were often shot.

Feeling Bradford probably had all kinds of unwitting accomplices in law enforcement, Cayman insisted no one in the law enforcement community could know of the escape plan but those few at the Bureau who'd put the plan in motion. If Emmett was caught, their window of opportunity was closed. They'd not be able to set up another escape and make it look like an escape.

The men filed into the yard, surprised by the extra time outside. Emmett's eyes darted to every corner of the yard, looking for a way to make a run for it. Some of the prisoners went to the tables and sat down, others roamed the yard, talking and visiting with other prisoners.

Emmett kept to himself, just as he always did. A prisoner approached him and bumped into him on purpose. *This must be it.* Emmett shoved back. A fight ensued. Emmett got in a few good punches before the guards broke them up. Both men were taken out of the yard and into separate solitary cells.

The guard shoved Emmett into his cell and shut the door, which was supposed to lock automatically. However, the guard stopped the door just a millimeter or two before it latched. Without so much as a second glance, the guard walked away, leaving the door slightly ajar. This was Emmett's moment.

Just inside his cell in a dark corner lay a guard's uniform. He quietly slipped into the uniform and, using the pillow from his bunk, quickly fashioned a fake 'Emmett' and covered him with the blanket. He wasn't sure it would fool anyone, but even it if gave him a few more seconds, it might mean the difference between discovery and escape.

He moved silently to the door, and pushed it open, very, very slowly. Was the guard in the hall? Had he gone back to his post outside the block? He stuck his head out very slowly and saw the hallway was clear. His heart pounding, he slipped out of the cell, walking silently to the end of the hall. The door to the stairwell was cracked open and he knew he was being given a path out of the prison. He followed it.

He'd only just placed his foot on the first step, when he heard guards coming up from the floor below. Trying not to panic, he ran to the left of the door, and into a short unlit hallway, hoping the darkness would provide enough cover to keep him from being discovered. The guards were talking to each other as they approached the top of the stairs and unlocked the door into the block.

"How's the fishing been this year? Have you been able to get out at all?"

"No, not yet. The kids have been sick and then the wife got sick. I've been working all day and tending sick family at night."

"I hear ya. We've had the same…."

The conversation was cut off as the two men proceeded through the door and it closed solidly behind them. He would have very few seconds to make it to the next open door. If they checked cells, he'd be discovered. With any luck at all, they were just passing through.

Emmett hurried down the stairs, afraid of meeting another pair of guards. There were none. He was nearing the main floor and none of the other doors had been left open for him. The next floors were basement and sub-basement levels and he continued down. Maybe there were tunnels down there he could use. The main door was locked and he continued down the stairs.

There were three doors leading into the basement section and one of them was unlocked. He moved cautiously through the unlocked door into what looked to be a storage room of some kind. Obviously not used often, there was dust everywhere, and dim lighting from three small windows across the top of one wall. Each window had bars on the outside of the frame, except the last one, which was slightly open.

Emmett's dark curly hair was soaked with sweat by this time. Thankful for his wiry runner's build at this point, he still barely managed to wriggle through the small window, checking the area outside before crawling out. It took him a minute to get his bearings, but he thought he was on the west side of the facility, near the freeway. He could hear the cars rushing by in the distance.

How was he going to get through the twenty-foot clearing that lay between him and the trees? He heard someone whisper his name and turned to see Agent Winston peering around the corner of the building, motioning for him to come. Emmett stepped into plain view, with as much authority as he could, using the full effect of the uniform he was wearing.

"My car is around the corner. Let's go."

"Where am I going?"

"I'm dropping you in D.C. and you're going to make your way to Bradford. You get to be his buddy for a few days. Hopefully, not longer than that."

Once inside the car, Emmett relaxed. He was a lousy actor, or so he'd been told in high school and he wasn't looking forward to trying to convince someone he was a guard. A ride out of the gate was a much better option. In the backseat, Emmett was covered with a blanket and lay on the floor. Winston placed empty boxes over him before proceeding through the gate.

Andre Winston flashed his ID at the gate guards and who waved him through without checking the car. Apparently no one had missed Emmett yet. About a mile from the prison, Emmett sat up and squirmed into the front seat.

"You wouldn't have brought me any street clothes, by any chance, would you?"

"As a matter of fact, I have. There's a bag in the back with clothes and toothbrush and paste, plus enough money for you to find a place to hole up, eat and get the things you might need that aren't in the bag. There's a cell phone in there, a computer with instructions for logging onto the private network. As soon as you get your cell phone charged, use this." Winston handed him a sim card. "That's what's going to hook you up with the Bureau. Cayman and Neo will be watching your every move."

"Sounds good to me. I hope this will all be believable enough for Bradford. He's NSA, you know. He's going to smell a set-up a mile away."

"As far as he knows, you've just escaped lockup. You were a troublemaker in there, picking fights and causing problems. Your hearing is set for next month, and you didn't want to wait around for them to convict you, so you told them all to kiss off and made a plan. The way the escape reads is your cell was found empty. No sign of your escape, no sign of you. They suspect you're still on the inside, waiting for your moment to run. That is the official story. You can slice it up as much as you want."

Andre was chuckling as he glanced at Emmett.
"What's so funny?"
"You'd make a lousy guard, Matisse. You're *way* too skinny." Emmett looked down at the pants he was wearing. In his hurry he hadn't noticed how baggy the pants were. The jacket didn't fit all that well, either.

"Yeah? Well, I might be skinny, but I'm scrappy. Just check my prison record."

Andre drove to a small alley behind some cheap restaurants. Emmett got out, opened the back of the SUV and pulled out his bag. "Wish me luck!"

He shut the back of the SUV and disappeared into the alley.

Epilogue

Emmett Matisse found a nice, quiet, out of the way, filthy motel just outside of D.C. and made himself comfortable. He needed to keep a low profile for a while. In truth, he needed a whole new profile. His new ID said his name was now Michael McPheeters. He thought about growing a beard, but there was hardly time and he was lousy at growing a beard anyway. He'd buy himself a beard, maybe some hair, then again maybe not some hair. Hopefully the beard would be enough with the right hat. Wigs made his head itch, and could always fly off in a stiff wind. If he couldn't make do with a fake beard by itself, he'd dye his hair.

Michael McPheeters sported sandy brown hair and a beard to match. Thanks to a new set of lenses, he now had green eyes. He'd had to try a couple of different hair colors to get just the right one, but it looked pretty good. The beard kit worked great and looked incredibly real. He was quite proud of his makeover.

A week passed since his escape and he was all over the news. Though that would definitely help legitimize his escape to Bradford, it left Emmett feeling a little exposed, so he decided it was time to move on. Once his disguise was in place, he moved to a new rat hole. He'd decided on a nicer motel, at least a step up from the previous filth, with monthly rentals. Emmett left his whereabouts in a dead drop at a predetermined park close to his motel.

On his last drop, he'd found a key wrapped inside a newspaper, and it looked remarkably like a car key. Returning to his motel, he found a note outside his room with a car attached. The note appeared to be from a woman of questionable employ wanting to hook up. Cayman always did have a great sense of humor.

When he was 'broke out of the big house', a line that still made him laugh, he'd been set up with everything he needed for the op. His 'kit' included money, fake IDs for his new identity, a cell phone, a list of dead drop locations for his updates to the Bureau, a laptop, disguises, and several small gadgets he would need to complete his mission.

During his time with Wesley Tipton, Emmett hadn't worked directly with Bradford, but his association with Tipton cemented a semi-relationship with Tristan Bradford. With Tipton dead, he'd use what information he'd gleaned from that relationship to form a new one with Bradford.

And so the search began…

To Be Continued…

Eradicated Preview
Book Five
Duty and Deception

Chapter One

Tristan Bradford had his arm firmly around Sophia's neck, his gun to her head. Neo pointed his gun at Bradford from fifty feet away, ready to take him out.

"Write it down. Write down the algorithm NOW and I let her live."

Neo calculated his odds, quickly and efficiently. Sophia had been threatening premature labor for nearly a week. If he were to shoot Bradford, he could scare Sophia into labor and the baby was a good nine weeks from their delivery date. If he didn't shoot, would Bradford really let her live? Bradford only wanted the algorithm for his own greedy purposes. For Neo, it was never about the money, it was always about making it available to everyone. He'd never written the formula down before, but now he had no choice.

Raising his gun over his head, he motioned with the other hand that he was reaching into the vest pocket of his body armor.

"I'm getting my notepad and pen. Don't shoot. I'm going to write it down."

Neo dropped his weapon to the ground and scrawled the information on the notepad. "See? Here it is. It's on the pad, now let her go." He tore the paper from the pad. "It's yours, as soon as you let her go."

Bradford released his terrified prisoner and she ran toward Neo. Suddenly, a shot rang out and Sophia's face changed from terror to sorrow. Her hand reached instantly to her belly and she staggered forward and fell to the ground.

"NOOOO!" Neo grabbed his gun from the ground beside him and ran to her, falling to his knees as another shot rang out. He felt the bullet enter just inside the armhole of his vest. As he fell to the ground he could hear an infant crying in the background and his body began moving side to side, side to side, side to side..."

"Neo! Neo! You're dreaming again. *Wake up*."

Neo gasp as air rushed into his lungs. He sat straight up in bed and grabbed Sophia with both arms holding her tightly. She stroked his back, whispering softly to him.

"It's okay, my love. It was just a dream. We're all okay." Sophia's voice was soft, gentle and reassuring. Neo could feel his body slowly relaxing.

He reached down with one arm and set his hand on her swollen belly.

Sophia stroked his face. "Was it the same nightmare?"

"Yes."

"Neo, I've never known you to have nightmares before. Even when I didn't know the work you did, you *never* had dreams like this."

"I know, I know. I'm not sure I understand it myself. But I've never had a new life involved in one of my ops before. I've always known, no matter what happens, I can protect us. But this dream makes me feel powerless to protect you and the baby. And this time, I heard him cry."

"You're going to protect us all, Neo, even Mrs. Barbosa. Between you and the rest of the Bureau, this baby won't be able to fill his diaper without the whole city of Washington D.C. knowing about it."

Neo chuckled softly. The two of them snuggled down into the blankets and Sophia rested her head on his shoulder, feeling the muscles in his arms flexing and relaxing. "Showoff," she murmured. Neo chuckled.

"Just making sure you understand the true depth of 'my guns.'"

Sophia giggled and snuggled in closer and in minutes she was back to sleep. She never complained when he woke her up with his nightmares. She was always worried about him, never about herself. He was amazed at how open she was with her love for him, and at how easily she shared herself with him. She was what he knew love to be. Sophia was going to be an amazing mother.

Neo lay in bed trying not to think about the dream, but there was something about it that always drew him in. There was something he was supposed to see, but he never could figure out what it was. And so he began, like so many nights previously, picking the dream apart to try and find that one 'something' he knew he was supposed to see.

The man was definitely Tristan Bradford. He was holding his wife at gunpoint. His was face evil, twisted, shining in the moonlight. He could never see Sophia's face, but he knew the woman was his wife. The setting…maybe it was the setting.

They were in a small clearing. It must have been at a park, because the grass they stood on was cut short by a mower. Around them there were trees…no…not trees. Around them there were bushes, large, full, green bushes.

Neo's eyes were closed now as he forced himself to examine the scene around them. He couldn't let himself look at Bradford or Sophia. They were frozen in place and he was able to move around them, seeing them in three dimensions. This was new. He'd never been able to see the whole scene before in 3D. Intrigued, he continued to push himself to focus on the scene around them, not on Sophia, quashing his fear for her life. All players in the dream were frozen in place, except for Neo, and now, he could reason with himself. He explained to himself he had no need to fear for his wife because this was just a dream.

The soft moonlight shone brightly on something in the bushes, a shoe, or a jacket arm. He looked closer and the image disappeared into the brush. He wanted to follow it, but he stopped. A feeling washed over him. Something told him he must *never* go into the brush. Never.

Neo's eyes popped open. It was dawn outside the windows and he wasn't sure if he'd slept or been awake as he walked his nightmare. Surely he couldn't have been asleep and talking to himself like he was awake, but it seemed like hours had passed since Sophia awakened him.

Moving the blankets slowly off of him so not to disturb her, he gently lifted her hand from his chest and kissed it softly, setting it on his pillow. He walked to the long windows and moved the curtain to the side, staring out onto the city. Was it smart to live in the fray? Should he have required Sophia and Mrs. Barbosa to leave and go into witness protection somewhere far away? No one would ever have found them in their island home had he not come back to D.C. to help Desmond. He didn't regret the decision to help his friend; he only regretted it revealed the hiding place of his family. Now he wondered if he could truly keep them safe.

The building they lived in was now a veritable fortress, thanks to the bureau. Entering the building required a retinal scan or fingerprint depending on the door that was entered. The only residences in the entire building were the penthouses, of which there were three. The remainder of the building was office space, which made it easier to monitor the comings and goings over that of hundreds of apartment dwellers. The penthouses in this building were put in when it was built to house foreign guests for a high finance company that since had gone belly up. The building owners decided to rent out the large apartments on the top floor and it worked out very well for Neo. The other two spaces were vacant, and would stay that way until Bradford was found. That made guarding Neo's penthouse all the easier. Still, Bradford had somehow managed to overcome two guards at the door and enter their unit unnoticed. Security was much tighter around the building for that reason. No such breaches had occurred since the security upgrade, and Neo felt much better about leaving his family where they were.

A shiver went down his spine and he turned to see his beautiful wife watching him.

"I thought you were asleep."

"I was, but how can I sleep when you're parading those cute buns all over the bedroom? Why waste a perfectly good view with sleep?"

She moved her hands over her head and a stretch traveled from her fingertips down her body, over her petite protruding belly and down her legs to her toes. He grinned watching her.

"That looked like it felt good."

"Mmmm," she said patting the empty place beside her. Come back to bed and snuggle me."

"You read my mind. Besides, my cute buns are cold." He pranced backwards, displaying his backside for Sophia to see. She laughed as he plopped down on the bed and cuddled in beside her.

"This is my favorite part of the day," she said, getting as close to him as she could.

"Oh, I don't know. I rather like riding in the SUV with Cayman."

Sophia jerked her head back, give him a mock angry look and slapped him playfully then nuzzled back in. Neo checked the time. It was approaching seven a.m. Sophia moved his face away from the clock.

"No, don't look at it. Just stay here with me today. We could play scrabble and watch Jeopardy. I'm so much better at Jeopardy than you are, and I could show off my smartness."

Neo laughed. "Oh, you think so? Well I highly doubt that you're better than I am. I say you start recording them, without watching the episodes mind you, and we'll just have to have a playoff. I'll make the popcorn."

"Oh good luck with making anything in *that* kitchen! Mrs. Barbosa will tan your hide if you tried that."

"Yeah? Well I'm bigger than she is and I can shoot a gun."

"Don't get cocky. She has a broom and she knows how to use it."

Neo gazed down at the woman he loved more than anything in the entire world. How could he love a child when all the love he had was poured into this one human being. He smiled at her.

"You know, you're pretty selfish."

Sophia started laughing and spoke through her laugher. "What brought that up?"

"Well, just look at you. You're hogging all my love and there's nothing left for our son. I'd say that was pretty selfish."

Sophia shook her head, her eyes glowing up at him. "You mean our daughter, of course, and just you wait. I've heard amazing things about how a parent can love."

"No, actually I mean our son, and I'll be the judge of that. I will tell you this, if it's a girl, I'm sending her back."

"You're hurting her feelings. She's crying now, ya big meanie. She thinks her daddy doesn't love her because she doesn't have a penis. How sad is *that*?"

"Oh, tell her to chill. I love you, after all and *you* don't have a penis. I've always known you were a little jealous of mine."

"And I thought I'd hid that so well." Sophia grabbed the spare pillow and began pummeling her husband with it.

"Hey! I'm just trying to be honest here."

Neo grabbed the pillow and pulled it from her hands, throwing it on the floor. He took her in his arms and lay her down on her pillow, covering her mouth with his. Every cell of her body responded to him.

They were interrupted by a knock on the door. It was Mrs. Barbosa.

"You be nice to Mrs. Neo!" she called through the door. "She a very delicate flower right now. No make me come in there!"

"Yes, Mrs. Barbosa," said Neo, stifling a laugh. "You're a 'delicate flower' now? Oh, if she only knew what you were capable of."

"Why," said Sophia breathlessly, "I have *no* idea what you're talking about. Really I don't."

Neo grabbed her and kissed her soundly. Sophia muffled a squeal; her smile prevented a solid kiss.

"Kiss me or you'll be stuck here all day."

In her best southern bell accent she said, "Oh, Mr. Neo, surely you wouldn't want to deprive this delicate flower of her nourishment? Now, would you?"

Neo released her and lay back in bed shaking his head. He rose and 'sauntered' into the bathroom. Sophia burst into laughter at his runway 'walk.'

Other books by JL Redington

Juvenile Series (8-13):

The Esme Chronicles:

A Cry Out of Time
Pirates of Shadowed Time
A View Through Time
A River In Time

Broken Heart Series:

The Lies That Save Us
Solitary Tears
Veiled Secrets
Softly She Leaves
Loves New Dawning

Passions in the Park:

Love Me Anyway
Cherish Me Always
Embrace Me Forever

Duty and Deception:
Novella Series

Erased
Entangled
Enlightened
Extracted
Eradicated

Come join me on
Facebook: Author JL Redington
Email: contact@jlredington.com
Twitter: @jlredington

Made in the USA
Charleston, SC
02 July 2015